SALT

SALT

A novel by Adriana Riva
Translated by Denise Kripper

velizbooks.com

La sal de Adriana Riva © 2019 Odelia Editoria

Salt © 2024 by Denise Kripper

All rights reserved. No part of this book may be used or reproduced in any manner whatsoever without written consent from the publisher, except for brief quotations for reviews.

Veliz Books titles are available to the trade through our website and our distributors, Small Press Distribution and Asterism.

For personal orders, catalogs, or other information, write to info@velizbooks.com

For further information write Veliz Books:
P.O. 1701, Houston, TX 77251, U.S.A.
velizbooks.com

ISBN: 978-1-949776-16-4

Cover image and front cover design by Sofía Galarce
Cover design by Silvana Ovaitt

Work published within the framework of "Sur" Translation Support Program of the Ministry of Foreign Affairs and Worship of the Argentine Republic. / Obra editada en el marco del Programa "Sur" de Apoyo a las Traducciones del Ministerio de Relaciones Exteriores y Culto de la República Argentina.

For mom

That's so strange! These mothers, curled up and hidden in the depths of our lives, at the very core of our lives, in the dark, so important, so influential over us! A person tends to forget about it in the course of living his life, or just doesn't give a damn. Or else you believe you don't give a damn, but you never stop giving a damn about any of it.

> Natalia Ginzburg
> Translated by Wendell Ricketts

Half of what I say is meaningless
But I say it just to reach you

> John Lennon

SALT

Translator's Note

01. The Fall

02. The Trip

03. The Birth

Acknowledgments

About the Author

About the Translator

Translator's Note

I read *La sal* almost as soon as it came out, almost in one sitting. Half on my train commute to work, half on the way back. I underlined it heavily and dog-eared many pages as I marked moving passages. One sentence towards the end of the book really stood out to me as a translator: "She looked up her whole life in dictionaries." The narrator is describing her mother, a character she feels both estranged from and drawn to. I understood all too well—translators are painfully aware of the limitations of dictionaries.

I recognized a certain affinity between the first-person narrator and myself: we are both from the same generation, from Argentina, from Jewish families. This is not a prerequisite for translating a work, but it was one of the reasons I started fantasizing about the prospect. Immediately, I felt I could channel the narrative voice in the novel because, in many ways, Adriana Riva and I were speaking the same language.

As chance would have it, when a couple of years later I actually did start translating the novel, there was another coincidence between the narrator and myself: we were both expecting. Pregnancy made me reconsider some of the questions at the core of the book about being a mother (how to mother a daughter?), and about being a daughter (how to be a daughter when you're a mother?).

Salt explores the complexities of intergenerational female family bonds.

A call from the past about a mysterious box marks the onset of the story as two pairs of siblings—the narrator and her sister, and their mother and aunt—go on a road trip. The perfect opportunity for the narrator to learn more about her mother's past, to rewrite their relationship.

Riva's literary story runs parallel to the narrator's need for a narrative. The family history folds onto itself: the return to the childhood home mimics the trip back to their place of origin, the construction of a new house counteracts the ruins of an old one, the hospital doubles as ER and maternity ward, characters take on different names for different lives. The way history repeats itself is germane to translation: there's always difference in repetition. Daughters might contain their mothers, but are not them. Some things resist reproduction.

The past tense pulses through the present narrative, returning as an echo. The narrator navigates this time warp, avoiding getting lost in translation in the search for an origin. Language acts as a narrative anchor, a family lexicon grounds them, Yiddish and Guarani make up part of this private universe. The similes are deliberately peculiar, a particular window into the quirks of this one family that could be anyone's family as well. Riva's intimate sketching makes her characters tridimensional, recognizable in all their flawed humanity—mothers and daughters as people.

Adriana Riva and I were speaking the same language. Literally. Born and raised in Buenos Aires, I have lived in the U.S. for many years. Spanish is my mother tongue. English, the language I became a mother in. I speak to my daughter in Spanish. I have an accent when I speak English. I hope readers can hear it in my translation.

01. The Fall

From December to March we spent our summers in the seaside city of Mar del Plata, in a big stone house that belonged to my paternal grandparents. On top of the mossy tiled roof, a Santa sleigh weathervane protected us from misfortune. It had been rusty for years, arbitrarily pointing East.

My sister Julia and I were always in charge of decorating the house for Christmas. We set up the tree next to the fireplace. It was a plastic eyesore, so scrawny it looked like one of those unremarkable poplars in the foothills. We spruced it up with an eclectic collection of ornaments: balls of different colors and sizes, a little one-eyed angel, a bright pink beat-up Star of David, a puppy inside a red stocking. The final touch was showering it with garlands and cotton balls. The cotton was key: it gave the illusion of being swaddled in snowy white, a cloak of happiness.

Next, we set up the manger inside the fireplace. The figures of Mary and Joseph belonged to the same set, but baby Jesus was larger than both his parents put together. There were also two Balthazars among the Three Wise Men. No one ever noticed; everyone looked at our collection and saw a manger—there was a general attention deficit at home.

Finally, we took the Christmas cards that came every year around the holidays and put them up on display. Most of them bore only the uninspiring signature of some manager, one of Dad's colleagues, but collectively they gave the impression of something important. Mom didn't help us at all, totally oblivious to tradition; instead of buying the customary turkey or vitel toné for our Christmas Eve dinner, she got ham and cheese ravioli.

Two days before a sticky hot Christmas, when we were about to start putting up the holiday greeting cards around the mantel, fireplace, and stairs, Julia announced she wasn't into it anymore. She was thirteen, two years older than me. She dropped the cards and disappeared down the hall. We had a communication problem, my sister and I. We used to pull each other's hair, scratch and spit at each other. We hated each other for days on end. When I yelled for her to come back she couldn't even be bothered to answer. I just took the cards and put them all up. Still annoyed by her insolence, I decided to surprise everyone with something special: using two leftover shiny garlands to decorate the sleigh weathervane.

I took the decorations and walked out of the garage, where there was always a ladder leaning against the wall. I started to climb. The hydrangeas surrounding the house shrank below me. With the wind, I thought, the garlands would turn the weathervane into a shooting star. I looked down the deserted street. There was only one car parked on the whole block: It was my mother's. The driver's window was open, and her elbow was poking out.

I kept on climbing. Behind the neighbor's hedge, a black Lab was sleeping on the grass. Outside the house across the street, a man in a muscle shirt was skimming the pool. Our roof was a lot higher than the others, but I wasn't afraid; I was excited about the change of perspective, pretending I was a giraffe. When I got to the top, I took a deep breath and with the back of my hand pushed my sweaty hair from my face. The wind brought a fishy stench from the coast that made me scrunch up my nose and all of a sudden the ladder started pulling away from the wall.

I clung to the sides in fear but realized too late that I was already falling backward. I let go and jumped, thinking I was closer to the ground than I actually was. I turned in mid-air, and my whole body smacked against the flagstones around the house. Later they told me it was a ten to fifteen-foot fall. The last thing I remember is a pale stray cloud in the sky and, far below, the fleeting look of my mother's face, inside the car, her jaw dropped, watching me fall—an image I've since tried in vain to process.

"Don't move, Ema. Please don't move," my mom told me when I came to, lying face-up on a hard bed, no pillow. I had been rushed by ambulance to a hospital in Buenos Aires.

"What happened?" I asked, my mouth dry. When I tried to turn my head to see where we were, I felt a jolt so intense that, before losing consciousness for the second time, I saw tiny stars flickering around me, like in cartoons.

When I came to again, my dad was holding my hand. I knew it was him before I even opened my eyes because I recognized his calloused and hairy fingers. He had the hands of a beast.

"Ema, I need you to be as still as a statue. I'll give you a quarter for every minute you don't move," he whispered in my ear. "Stay put...stay, stay," he said as if speaking to a pet. Once he was sure I had understood, he explained that I had crushed three dorsal vertebrae: the third, under the shoulder blades, the sixth, a little bit below that, and the eleventh, right where I'd have breasts someday.

"What is dorsal?" I wanted to know. Dad found a piece of paper somewhere in the room and drew a bunch of horizontal lines, one under the next, in a column. Those lines were the vertebrae that made up the spine, he explained, the structure holding my skeleton. Three were damaged. He highlighted them to indicate they were broken. On top of those horizontal lines, he drew a long, vertical one—my spine. He smeared a few little lines around it to signify that it was swollen. By the time he was finished drawing, all I saw were menacing hieroglyphics, and I felt even more lost than before.

As he spoke, I glanced at the room around me, moving my eyes from one corner to the other like a cuckoo clock, trying to make sense of my new reality. The pain had faded along with my clarity. I felt blurry. At times, I dissociated and saw myself from impossible angles. Years later, I learned I was given IV morphine.

"And that's why you can't move, Ema, not even a little bit. Not until this line in the center gets better," Dad said, pointing with the pen to my spine. Before leaving, he kissed me on the forehead and gave me a pinch on my chin.

Deciphering the meaning of "dorsal" was my one obsession during those first days of convalescence. Little by little I came to learn that and a few more things, through half-heard whispers, the hoarse voices of doctors responding to the tense voice of my mother somewhere in the room. Because of this constant whispering, in my nightmares I swapped witches and ghosts for paraplegics and amputees, uncertain of the kind of monster I was up against.

The orthopedic surgeon checked in every afternoon, poking my feet and legs. He smiled every time I said it hurts, it hurts. I named him the Tin Man. He never offered me a lollipop or a kind word, but I later found out he traveled all around the country telling my story at conferences and collecting enough diplomas to plaster the walls of his office. My accident had been labeled exceptional—it was a miracle I wasn't paralyzed.

The first two nights I spent in the hospital, Mom stayed with me, sleeping on a chair I couldn't see because I couldn't move my neck. I know there was also a window somewhere because nurses opened it daily to air out the room, though they couldn't really get rid of the smell of iodine and lethargy stuck in my mouth. My vision was limited to the moon-like white ceiling, where water stains turned into mice, birds' beaks, and mouthless faces. These were my imaginary friends during my hospitalization.

On the third night, when she was told again that it was not possible to provide an extra bed for overnight stays, Mom went home to sleep and sent Juvencia instead, a Paraguayan maid who had started working for us three weeks before. It was she who endured sleepless nights on a chair without armrests while I was in the hospital. Her only comfort was a pillow the night nurses smuggled in for her, which she had to secretly return every morning.

Juvencia was stocky, with dark skin and frizzy hair. Her brown eyes were the size of the marbles my cousins kept in a jar. I don't know what kind of clothes she wore because I only ever saw her in the blue uniform with white polka-dots that fit tightly around her hips. Whenever someone entered the room she hurried to put on her flip-flops. The rest of the time she preferred being barefoot.

She spoke to me in Guarani with a sweet smile, like a guava fruit. *Che mitãkuña, che mitãkuña*, she'd say, *my girl, my girl*. That's what she called me from day one. Every morning she washed me for hours with a damp cloth that now and then she twirled with her chubby arms. All the while she whistled a calming mantra, but I couldn't surrender to the ritual. Her touch between my legs, my thighs, and armpits made me uncomfortable. I wasn't used to physical contact. Mom had never hugged me. Dad wouldn't even put his arm around me for a picture. We were like a family of bowling pins. I put up with this ceremony for two weeks until I finally asked Mom to please tell Juvencia not to take so long cleaning me. She blushed.

"I specifically asked her to do it like that so the morning would go by faster. I thought you'd like it."

"I don't. Just ask her for a quick wash, please," I begged her. From then on, the bath took ten minutes.

Mom and Dad had decided against putting me through surgery. They were suspicious of shortcuts, so my recovery took the longest road: casting and waiting. The former happened three weeks after my admission into the hospital when the doctors burst into my room waving an X-ray and proclaiming loudly: "The swelling went down!" To put the cast on, they took me on a gurney to another room, where they hung me vertically from a harness while a crowd of white coats inspected me. I felt the dissociation of the first days again. It was as if I was seeing myself from the opposite corner of the room. What I saw was a life-size puppet being covered in bandages and plaster. I felt high, happy; the cast meant that I'd be able to leave the hospital in a few days. But when they took me back to my room, I first saw my reflection not in a mirror, but in my mother's eyes. She was crying in horror. She had to cover her mouth with her hand to hide the tremor in her lips. She hadn't understood the armor would cover me from top to bottom, including my head. Only my face and arms were bare. A mummy in a sleeveless shirt.

"It's okay, Mom, I'm fine," I comforted her.

It didn't work. There was no way to cheer her up. A malignant growth of denial had been developing in her for many years.

The first few hours in my new breastplate were asphyxiating. It was hard to breathe. Neither my throat nor my belly had enough space for the seesawing movement. I had to concentrate to avoid atrophying a mechanism as natural as inhaling and exhaling. The Tin Man said it was a matter of getting used to it and that I was mature enough to get these things. These things,

I would have liked to tell him, take years to "get," but I only learned that a lot later.

It took days for the cast to dry. It was cold inside and it froze my spirits. Even today, I still remember that icy chill and think of Juvencia, with the hairdryer she had borrowed from her mother-in-law's salon to warm me up. *Che mitãkuña, che mitãkuña.* Damp both day and night, I experienced the dread of the interminable. I couldn't sleep or think of anything except wonder how long one could live like this and what it would be like to die with my eyes open. Then one morning I suddenly realized the dampness was gone and I was discharged. When I was leaving the hospital, just before they put me in the ambulance, lying on the stretcher, I managed to see the treetops and the sky. I cried for the first time since my fall, moved by the beauty we take for granted. With my mouth wide open, I took a big gulp of fresh air, and tears ran down my temples and disappeared inside the cast that covered my hair.

At home I was placed in my room, where they put a TV on top of a pile of boxes so that I could comfortably watch the screen. Julia, who shared the room with me, was moved to the study so she could carry on with her schedule and school routine. Juvencia moved in, but was far from us, in the utility room, behind the washing machine and in front of the clothesline. It was a windowless room, with just enough space for a bed and a small nightstand, where she put up her Saint Expeditus praying cards.

"Are you happy to be back home? Things will be easier now," Mom said caressing my arm. She was wearing a perfume that smelled of spring.

"Here, right next to your bed, is a buzzer to call us if you need anything."

I smiled. I wanted to ask her to sit down and tell me a story, but I didn't know how. She proceeded with her instructions:

"See? You press here and it rings in Juvencia's room. She'll be available to you 24/7."

"Thanks, Mommy," I answered. She kissed my forehead and left. She had things to take care of. My discharge and all the hospital paperwork had taken longer than expected, and now she was running late for a lot of things.

As soon as she left, I felt like Mom was a colossal stone with the gravity of an entire planet pulling me in and weighing on my chest. Imagining it was a detonator that could destroy her, I pressed the buzzer over and over until I heard the sound of Juvencia's flip-flops coming.

The recovery at home took four months, three of which I spent horizontally, without moving from the bed except when transported by an ambulance to go in for X-rays to check on the progress of my vertebrae. Juvencia used those mornings to change the sheets that reeked of sweat and piss and body grease. While prostrate, my hygiene was almost nonexistent. Every morning, when the sun reached the bed, she came in with a quiet whistle and a lukewarm, dampened cloth so I wouldn't get cold, but my hair, trapped under that plaster helmet, wasn't washed for months. When I had to pee, Juvencia placed the bedpan between my legs and then left me alone so I could relieve myself without being embarrassed. On top of the jumble of bandages, I wore a cotton nightgown with panda bears that wasn't getting washed either. And the filth kept piling up until it almost became part of the room, like a black cat curled up in a corner.

On average, I watched three films a day, and I eventually learned the words to *The Sound of Music* by heart.

"I get a fiendish delight thinking of you as the mother of seven. How do you plan to do it?"
"Darling, haven't you ever heard of a delightful little thing called boarding school?"
"I always try to keep faith in my doubt, Sister."
"After all, the wool of a black sheep is just as warm."

The most complicated thing about my horizontal life was swallowing. I did it using a blue plastic tube filled with squash puree or apple smoothies and sweet chocolate milk, which Juvencia prepared with tons of cornstarch mixed in with warm milk to prevent me from losing more weight. I never asked for a mirror, but my aunt Sara, my mother's only sister, used to call me "raisin" every time she visited.

Julia brought me letters from my classmates. They came in envelopes decorated with stickers and spelling mistakes, and offered a catalog of irrelevant news:

"I'll tell you a secret: I don't like Sebastián anymore, now I like Felipe. He's sooo cuuuute but kinda short."
"I bought a jean jacket just like yours."

"UR gonna miss my bday party, it's gonna be awesome."

"Its time for my pottery class, gotta go. Your amazing, XO!"

At first, my sister brought tons of letters that she read to me so we could spend time together without her getting bored, but because I didn't want to answer any (I couldn't do it myself, and I didn't want to dictate them to anyone, let alone my sister), the piles of letters quickly dwindled to a few here and there, to eventually none.

Visits were scarce. Two or three friends came and talked more amongst themselves than to me. Lying down, I could barely even see their profiles, and I became an expert in enjoying fleeting moments. I filled my days with trivial things: the fresh air of the early morning, the cotton particles floating against the cream-colored light, the smell after the rain.

When my friends got closer to say goodbye, the sight of their faces was as unsettling as a Picasso painting. Their noses were getting bigger before the rest of their faces and some started developing acne on their foreheads. Those mutations were the irrefutable proof that while I couldn't go back to who I was, nor yet turn into something else, the world kept evolving without me.

From those visits, one in particular is engraved in my memory: the afternoon Ana came to visit, the only one of my friends who dared to come alone. The night before, she had been grounded for cutting a lock of her hair, so our visit was almost canceled. But because her parents were religious and visiting me was almost charity, they allowed it in the end. Ana had long straight hair like the kind you see in shampoo commercials or that's sold to make wigs, but that afternoon when she came, there was a hole in her bangs as if she were missing a tooth. Because I couldn't see it properly, I asked her to stand on my bed, right around my feet. From my horizontal position I watched her making silly faces celebrating her audacity, and I burst into tears.

It was the second and last time I cried during my convalescence. Ana got uncomfortable and asked me if she had inadvertently hurt me or if something was wrong. I told her it was nothing, I was just emotional, that's all. But I was actually crying because I had caught a glimpse of her bra under her school shirt. I felt like a caged creature, forgotten, confined to this plaster monstrosity that was keeping me from growing, and I felt anger and self-pity. I wanted breasts, too. I wanted things I couldn't even name.

That night, Juvencia noticed I was so sad that her eyes filled with tears, but she was such a proud woman that she didn't let on. She spent the entire night with me, whispering in my ear an endless story about a fox in a reed bed, repeating like a ballad some phrases that even today I still remember by heart: *Poraviomosarambikavaju para, hákatuñandeha'eñaínañaha'ãva* (destiny shuffles the cards, but we are the ones who must play the game).

The day they finally took off my cast, the Tin Man used an electric saw that made my mom, who never asked too many questions, inquire about how far that thing was going to go. When the teeth of the blade started to spin, I closed my eyes and repeated to myself the only tongue twister I knew by heart. *Peter Piper picked a peck of pickled peppers, a peck of pickled peppers Peter Piper picked.* After a few minutes that seemed endless amid the dust that floated in the air, the doctor used a pair of scissors to cut off the last bandages still stuck to my skin with the indifferent enthusiasm of a mayor in a ribbon-cutting ceremony. "That's it, we're done," he suddenly said, and he left me alone with my stunted body, while he and my mom went back to murmuring somewhere in the room.

My first feeling of freedom was tempestuous. I breathed deeply, inflating my chest, and an unknown pain shot through my ribcage; I felt like a defenseless turtle whose shell had just been removed. For a moment I was about to beg the Tin Man to put me back in my cast. After a few hours though, I was feeling better and already trying to recover the countless movements that had atrophied over so many months.

Against doctor's orders, as soon as I got home, I asked to be seated. I needed verticality, but the dizziness was so bad that Juvencia had to help me lie down while Mom, at the door, cried in distress. Even though they had promised as much since day one, she still didn't believe that I'd ever walk again.

A week later, when I could sit without feeling a wave of nausea, I asked Juvencia to help me stand. I hadn't been on my feet in six months, and the pain was so intense I let out a guttural scream, which terrified Mom.

"What's wrong?" she asked without wanting to know.

I told her I felt as if I had put the entire weight of my body on my nose. She didn't ask anything else. She was on her way out of my room when Juvencia told her she could get me some horse ointment. Mom gave her an astonished look. Juvencia explained to her that it wasn't uncommon, that it was something her relatives in Paraguay used after walking barefoot on hot coals during celebrations, yes ma'am, a salve used on racehorses' hooves, as a pain reliever, yes ma'am, sold in stores, not the street, and with that, the girl will be able to stand, and Mom, nervously, hurried to answer sure, Juvencia, buy it and I'll reimburse you.

A few days later, thanks to the miraculous salve, I started taking my first steps. When I could finally walk on my own without Juvencia's hand on my back, we went out for dinner to celebrate. She didn't come. By the end of the year, she was gone. Mom said something about not liking the way Juvencia looked at her. Even nowadays I think it was in that moment that my childhood ended: not the day of my fall, nor the first time I wore a bra, but the day Juvencia said goodbye with a last *che mitãkuña* and left me there alone, with a jumbled and dirty head of hair, still cocooned in the body of a girl.

02. The Trip

When I'm about to go on a trip, the smell of toasted bread and freshly made coffee makes me uneasy, and I wish for a sedentary life. It's something I inherited from Mom; traveling makes her anxious. When she arrives at the destination, she doesn't know what to do. All she really wants is to go home.

A moment ago, I found her reading the newspaper in the dining room, still sleepy, drinking her first morning coffee with two sweeteners. She was eating wheat toast, breaking it apart with her hands on a chipped plate. She has almond-shaped acrylic nails, the hands of an attractive woman. She's always enjoyed eating with her hands. Citrus fruits especially, that leave her fingers all sticky and unusable, holding them up in the air until she can wash them. I'm old enough to have a few gray hairs myself, but she still tries to peel an orange for me every chance she gets. She removes the rind piece by piece until the fruit is bare, leaving its bittersweet wrapper all over the plate. Other things, however, she hates sharing. As a kid, I always asked her for a bite of her toast, which was invariably tastier than mine. She shared warily, like whenever my son Antonio asks me for that last piece of chocolate I haven't managed to wolf down in time. While I have tried hard to be different, I am like her—daughters inevitably contain their mothers.

I take a scalding shower and go to my mother's bedroom. She is still not dressed. She's wearing a pink satin nightgown, sleeveless with a plunging neckline that exposes her pigeon chest. It protrudes; a bone malformation she hides under fur coats. She keeps so many secrets that she's ended up inflated from the inside, like one of those fancy Mylar balloons that party stores sell for twenty times the price of regular ones because they don't pop.

She's finishing up her packing.

"Are you almost done? I'm ready," I tell her.

It's cold in her bedroom. Mom is not wearing any makeup. She has rosacea and dry skin that has been flaking off for years. No facelift can stop time. Her hair, ever since I can remember, has always been a whitish color, a cloak of strong and straight gray hair that barely covers her ears. Her gray hair is the only thing she has never hidden.

"You know what?" she replies, oblivious to the fact that we're in a rush. "I think these are Antonio's best years and he doesn't even know it. Then one day he'll grow up, lose the ability to forget, and it's all downhill from there."

Her head is somewhere else, in a place I can't access. It's because of the trip, I think.

"Sara doesn't think so. She says it's not true. For her, the best years are childhood and adolescence, as well as one's forties and seventies. But I'm always going to be 'sweetie' to her, the pessimistic baby sister. For me, it's all rotten, even being young. My good years were the ones I spent with your father because he made everything feel complete. But it wasn't thirty-five years of love; it was thirty-five years of understanding. I was exactly what your father wanted."

She says it with a laugh to downplay the drama, and I go along. I respond with a meaningless click of the tongue. Outside, daylight begins to break, and mist fogs up the window facing the avenue.

A few weeks ago was the first anniversary of my father's death. We gave away all his Italian suits and French ties and English shirts. But in the bedroom, from the valet stand, still hangs a silver robe de chambre, worthy of an all-powerful king. In the drawers and wardrobe, there's still a lot to get rid of. For months now, Mom manages to get in the mood and fill two or three trash bags, only to quickly abandon the crusade, overwhelmed by memories. The bags stay piled up in the laundry room. It's hard, leaving no trace of an entire lifetime.

A meringue-looking duvet covers the bed. Only Mom's side is wrinkled. The other, disquietingly perfect.

"Have you said goodbye to Lucas and Antonio?" she asks me, holding a pair of pantyhose in each hand.

"Not yet. I'll do that now and then we'll leave. Hurry up, the others are waiting."

The others are my sister Julia and my mother's sister Sara. I like to think of us being on one side and them on the other. But these are fictional sides, they only exist in my imagination. Bonds are circumstantial.

Today, the four of us are driving to Macachín, the town in La Pampa where my mother and Sara were born. The idea came to me after my father's death, when I realized that not only are my memories of him eroding, but so is everything about Mom's past, like Paraná delta islets floating rivers apart.

———————

I started taking anxiety medication two months after my father's funeral, following dreams that I had lost my wallet with my ID and credit cards inside and that the car I was driving kept running through all the red lights. Those were days of intense humidity and smelly cigarettes. And then one morning, Antonio climbed into my bed, put his ice-cold feet inside the sheets and, lifting my eyelids, asked me to tell him about his grandmother. There was a note from the teacher asking parents to help their kids with writing their family history. By family, Antonio had understood "Grandma Elena." He didn't remember Grandpa Ignacio anymore.

I told him what I knew. That Mom was born in Macachín, a remote town in the remote province of La Pampa, so ridiculously close to Buenos Aires where at the end of the nineteenth century her grandparents had arrived from Ukraine along with so many other starving Jews. That the train tracks divided the town in two: on one side the Jews, on the other the Germans. That the town had a bare plaza possessed by swirling clouds of dust; a school where his Grandma Ele and his Aunt Sarita were forced to read Eva Perón's autobiography; and a synagogue, to honor the Sabbath. His great-grandfather Abraham ran the corner dry goods store. I didn't realize the caricature I was painting. I told him that Grandma liked telling the story of one of her uncles who at fifteen, got on a train after leaving a note that said "I will earn my bread by the sweat of my brow" only to be forced off at the following station.

"What is remote?" Antonio interrupted.

I didn't know how to answer. That question or any question. Then we got up and moved to the desk where, in his impressively round handwriting, Antonio wrote in his notebook what I had told him.

He asked for more. I told him that when they were still quite young they moved to Buenos Aires to go to college. His great aunt Sara came first to study law, then his grandmother, my mom, medicine. They lived on Vicente López Street. "Vicente López and Ayacucho," they said, despite actually being closer to Vicente López and Junín. Now on that street there's a hideous movie theater complex where I take Antonio to see loud cartoons. Back then, it was a legendary tenement block full of Romanies.

"What do you mean Vicente López and Ayacucho?" he asked. He had turned eight the week before.

I was actually telling the story to myself, but to avoid losing him, I told him that he had inherited his curly hair from Grandma.

"But Grandma doesn't have curly hair!" he replied without even looking up, concentrating on his notebook.

She does, but I've never seen it either. Every week for over fifty years, Mom has been getting her hair done at Pino Style. She goes in with wet hair, which she covers with a transparent shower cap that has embarrassed me since I was Antonio's age. She has never showed her curls to anyone. Not even when she traveled to Jordan with Dad to see the lost city of Petra and found out, once there, that the salon inside their five-star hotel was closed. To prevent her hair from becoming a frizzy nest, she bribed the bellhop and concierge and got into a black car like the ones sheiks use in American films. She crossed half a desert and arrived at a cave where three women in burqas straightened her hair.

The day Mom read what Antonio had written—what I had dictated to him—she gave me a surprised look. We were sitting around the blue kitchen table amidst a pervasive smell of hot milk.

"That's wrong. It didn't happen like that," she said. She was staring at me with her bright eyes—a color I could never define. "That's not my story. You don't get it."

To appease my anger, I lifted my chin a bit and my eyebrows slightly and asked her to tell me how things had really happened.

She started by saying the plaza was not dusty nor bare but green and full of people like any other. That no one forced them to read Evita, but that they did it out of their own conviction because everyone supported Perón. And that her town had the same dramas and joys as any other place on the planet. She snorted almost to herself, stretching her lips, and then chuckled long enough that it became a conciliatory laugh. It was only then she admitted that, so very long after having left the town, now seeing it from the outside, she had inadvertently distorted it. The same had happened to her Jewishness. All of her acquaintances back then were Jewish. There was nothing wrong with being Jewish.

"And it wasn't such a remote town. We were Jewish is all. Also, we didn't call ourselves 'the Jews'; if anything, we called ourselves 'yidn,'" she corrected me.

The shame came later, when something or someone—she doesn't know when—caused her to start saying the word "Jew" in a lower voice for fear of having to explain something others couldn't understand.

Mom became quiet, and the ticking of the clock on the wall deepened the silence. She looked at me with her back very straight—and admitted it.

"The Petra story was dead on."

I go to the room where Antonio is sleeping, uncovered and belly-up. I stroke his hair and place one curl behind his ear. The floor is scattered with toys. When he was a baby, I spent hours watching him breathe; I thought I could consume him by staring at him. Then I got over it.

I'm now pregnant for the second time. It isn't the right moment to have another child. That moment flew by while I was overwhelmed with Dad's illness. It came and went, and after months of pleading, I finally gave in to Antonio's demand (who had been adding one or two brothers in soccer jerseys to his family drawings since before kindergarten) and to Lucas's whim (who always dreamed of having two boys). I caved one starless night of slanting drizzle. Now the family is expanding at the wrong time. I always check the watch on my left wrist to see how long things take, so this asynchronicity poses an existential problem for me.

Two months ago, we sold our apartment and moved back to my childhood home to live with my mom until the end of the year while we renovate our new place.

Living in this house is like living in my own time warp. Lucas and I sleep in the study, where the fluorescent lighting buzzes like a beehive. Antonio sleeps in my old room, with the bed right next to the window, which at night lets in wind, cold, and monsters.

Lucas asked me to wake him before going, but I leave him a note instead. He went to bed late. He just opened a brewery with a couple of his friends, and they take turns working the night shift.

"Should we have another coffee before we go?" asks Mom. Having a coffee is her excuse to delay the day, her life. She lives for those coffee breaks.

"No, we can stop on the way there. Julia just told me they're waiting for us."

We get in the car. I'm driving.

"Four blew me off this week," Mom tells me at the first stoplight. She's leaning her head back, her eyes closed halfway.

"What do you mean 'four'? Four what?"

I think of the fairy tale "The Brave Little Tailor," who killed seven at one blow.

"They gave me the cold shoulder; I know they were ignoring me. I was going to go with Clara Unzué to the Anchorena anniversary party, but she didn't even call me to cancel. She stood me up. There I was, waiting like a fool. It was Cuqui Anchorena's party. When she found out I knew about it, she tried to play it off and wrote to me saying that of course they were counting on my attendance. Then, Carlitos. Can you believe it? Carlitos, of all people. After the art opening, they all went to his place for a drink and didn't tell me about it. I went to the movies on my own instead. And the fourth, I don't remember... Oh, yes, of course, Miguel Otero, the reporter. I saw him at Teresa's tea party. The three of us were talking, and when Teresa stood up to say hello to someone, he took off after two minutes and left me talking alone. I was stunned, I couldn't believe it."

"There's a plot against you..."

"You bet there is."

Since Dad passed, Mom has been waiting to be banished to Siberia by the high society she has rubbed shoulders with for the past thirty-five years. She's waiting for the thumbs down, for the guillotine, for the phone to stop ringing, for the end of the invitations to art openings, benefit dinners, anniversary celebrations. All her life she has been confused about who she is.

"I think you are exaggerating a bit. I'm sure there's another explanation."

"But there isn't. In fact, the devil's in the details. That's where truth lies. Or don't you think that if Clara Unzué had stood Muni Álzaga up she wouldn't have called the next day to apologize?"

"I don't understand why you care so much about these things."

"Life is all about give and take, and I don't have anything to give now."

There are almost no cars out. Three girls with their hair, eyes, and lips painted black run across the street. They laugh when they get to the other side.

"When your father was alive, I could wear heels because I had him to hold on to. Now I could twist my ankle at any moment. I don't have anyone to lean on."

I would like to tell her that she has me, that she can lean on me, but she's not interested in me in that way. I don't know what she sees when she looks at me.

On the third day after moving into my mother's place, I woke up and she wasn't there. After a work meeting, at lunchtime, I set the table for the two of us and waited for her. She never showed. Antonio came back from school at quarter past five, and Lucas arrived as it was getting dark. I also set a place for Mom at dinner. I called her cellphone. Twice. She didn't answer. We ate without her, cutlets with mashed potatoes, prepared by the part-time maid that has been helping her since Dad died.

As Antonio played with his food, turning it into a volcano, he told me he had a birthday party the next day. I told him that when I was a kid, my mom always picked me up last from parties. I waited for her sitting in a corner, staring at some fries mushed on the floor, orphaned balloons detaching from the walls, and the birthday girl's mother, now finally enjoying a piece of dry cake. I waited for Mom with my toes pointing in, one tip on the other, in the most absolute silence so no one would notice I was still there, all the while imagining an accident with so much blood that it would cloud my sight. At last, right before they turned off the lights, she showed up with her giant sunglasses, her long blue nylon jacket, and her clutch under her arm, and asked me if I had a good time. I gave her the silent treatment. We took the elevator down in silence, got in the car in silence, and then I spent the entire ride back home doodling with my finger on the car window like I didn't have a care in the world.

"I don't think you were always last to be picked up. It was probably just one time that's now etched in your mind," Lucas cut me off, his mouth full of flan.

Maybe he was right. How many times can the past be repeated?

I changed the topic and talked about work, about the design meeting I had that morning.

"We're working on a new kids' puzzle of Argentina, but with more pieces and illustrations about our indigenous peoples. Do you think kids would like it?"

"I don't know, like the Wichí people, you mean?" he answered without even looking at me, fishing flan bits and eating them straight from the serving dish. He always ate voraciously. He's the type of person who will stick his fork into a disproportionately large piece of chicken with not one, not two, but three fries, a good amount of mayo, some mustard, a bit of lettuce, and then try to fit the entire thing right into his mouth, flapping his nostrils and forcing his jaws to eat it all in one mouthful.

Lucas opened his full mouth and showed it to Antonio, who imitated him. They laughed together. After clearing up the table, I saved Mom a plate of food in case she came back later. A bit before midnight, I called her once more. She picked up as I was about to leave her a third message.

"Hello… I cwan't twalk. Cwall Sawita."

"Mom, are you okay? What's wrong? Where are you?"

"Awll gwood. Cwall Sawita."

Mom hung up the phone, and my heart started beating faster. I thought of Dad in his final days—his mouth violently open, his cracked tongue, and his inability to form words. I felt like I was being swallowed by a black hole again.

I called Aunt Sara.

"Mrs. Sara is not here," answered Basilia, with that provincial accent I loved imitating as a kid because it was one of the few things I could do better than Julia.

"And Mom? Is she there, Basilia?"

"No, Mrs. Elena is not here either."

I called my aunt's cellphone. Eight times, until she picked up. She was at the theater.

"Sorry, honey, I should've called you. It's nothing. Don't worry about it. Your mom is at home."

Months before, Mom had gone to the doctor because something was bothering her in her mouth. They did a biopsy and it came back benign. Had that menacing tissue come back? Why couldn't she talk right when I spoke to her? Once again, the fear, the feeling of landing on GO TO JAIL in a game of Monopoly.

"But what happened, Sarita? Please…"

"Nothing, it's silly. Your mom needed some dental implants and her face is all swollen, so she didn't want to see anyone."

Mom has a smile of a thousand teeth, all fake, blindingly white, covering an old rot I have never seen. According to her, everyone in her town had bad teeth because of the water. Many times, I imagined her going to school with classmates all dressed in spotless smocks who, when opening their mouths to answer the teacher, displayed a set of black and sharp teeth. Once, eating corn on the cob in the dining room, she suddenly stopped, put her hand on her mouth, and ran off to the nearest dentist.

The relief of knowing Mom didn't have a terminal illness didn't last long. A wave of rage took over me, tensed my guts, muscles, nerve endings. It rose to my face and exploded in a burst of hot lava behind my eyes. She could have told me she had a dental appointment. Left a note that she wasn't coming back for dinner, or to sleep, or something. I wanted to scream in her face that she was an awful mother, just awful, who ruined everything, but it was Sara on the other end of the line, not her. She's never there. I held my cellphone against my chest to muffle the sound and be able to scream loudly, very loudly, as if trying to give birth to my own mother. Instead, I breathed in deeply until I calmed down.

"I almost had a heart attack, Sarita. How could you not tell me about this?"

"You're right, dear, but what's done is done. She will be staying with me for a few days until the swelling goes down."

I hung up in that pathetic way we do now, with a swipe on my phone. I couldn't even end the conversation forcefully, smashing the receiver against the device. I went to the kitchen, took the plate I had saved for her, and threw the food in the trash. Mom only trusts two people, and I am neither of them. Dad is dead and now

Sara is her only protector. I drank a huge glass of Coke and with my teeth nicely coated in sugar, I went to bed. Before falling asleep, I felt the baby moving inside me. It was doing somersaults. I put my hand on my belly trying in vain to calm him down. I had it coming.

The following morning, calmer, I sent a text message to Mom to see how she was feeling, and another one to Julia, to know if she was aware of the situation.

"Classic Mom," answered Julia. "I'll give her a call later."

"Everything's all right, I'll call you tomorrow," wrote back Mom.

Two more days went by in which I hardly exchanged messages with her. Julia hadn't managed to see her. "Can you believe she doesn't want to see me either?" she texted, as if she had higher daughter status than me.

She does have it; it's not true parents love their children equally. Though they aren't really friends, Mom and Julia are confidants. They look for and find one another, they tell each other things. For years my mother has been telling my sister she needs to get liposuction in her legs. Julia answers that she looks great in pants and to leave her alone. Mom tells her that since Dad died she has been depressed, Julia tells her she wants a boyfriend, Mom tells her she is also looking for a boyfriend, Julia looks at her with a mocking face, Mom insists she deserves a boyfriend, Julia laughs in disbelief, Mom tells her something is bothering her in her mouth and that she's worried, Julia tells me when the biopsy results come back negative.

Mom doesn't feel comfortable when she's alone with me. She looks at me like a mother looks at her child in a school play, proud of what belongs to her in some way, but also somewhat alienated, like when she first saw the mole that had grown in my armpit, just out of her reach. "Where did this come from?" She doesn't hug or kiss me; she just touches my arm occasionally with her ballerina hands.

Four days after her disappearance, she called me.

"I have something to tell you."

What you cannot say straight is always disruptive: a death, an illness, a pregnancy. For an instant I experienced the deafening silence that precedes transcendental moments.

"I didn't get dental implants. I had plastic surgery done."

I tightened my jaw, counted to ten, got up to thirty, and only then was I able to let go. Lying gets a hold of the both of us. It's the disguise we wear daily, allowing us to slip away into the nearest gutter to avoid confrontation. Sometimes they're absurd lies, saying we were reading when in fact we were taking a nap. Doing nothing is frowned upon. But in general, I'm amazed by the ease with which I can feign feelings with her. There is no boundary between truth and lies in our relationship.

"What did you get done, Mom?" I asked, my voice rotting with disappointment, not really wanting to know.

She couldn't say precisely. "Just something around my eyes and my double-chin." A new face. "I felt old in front of the mirror. You'll understand when you're my age. It's exasperating. Sometimes I think I'd rather die than age poorly. Well, than age, period. There's no such thing as aging well."

"Don't be so dramatic, youth goes by so quickly. You taught me that," I reminded her.

"Did I say that?"

"Yes. 'Youth is but an effervescent tablet,' that's what you said."

What I like best about Mom's face are her cheekbones, those two shoulder pads of bones that rise below her eyes to give her a distinguished bearing. Her wide forehead and straight nose are also perfect. It's a face that instills peace, elegance—the opposite of my boring and totally ordinary face. "You don't look anything like your mother," people tell me not without pity when they look at me. I smile without showing my teeth. My face is impossible to remember. It's not even ugly. I would have liked to look like her, but that's not how life works. I didn't choose my face, nor my parents, nor my upbringing, nor my date of birth, nor the accident that kept me away from the world for six months. I hung up, and again I felt the same coil of fear that, since Dad's death, fastens me to life.

That afternoon, unannounced, I went to Sara's. Basilia opened the door and let me into the living room, where I waited for my new mother to show up. When I saw her, I didn't know how to disguise the shock. Her face was covered in purple bruises, blood clots squeezed under a synthetic skin. Her eyes hiding at the back of her skull, so tiny they wouldn't even be able to distinguish a guinea pig from her daughter. Her mouth, still muzzled by the pain of the surgery and the medication, barely moved.

"You look all right, I was expecting worse," I said.

She had trouble speaking. She said the total recovery time would be three weeks. We drank some water; she didn't want to eat anything. Then I told her I had to go, that I had only stopped by to give her a kiss. But I didn't kiss her. On my way down in the elevator, I felt that she was more distant than ever. When I got home, I made myself some tea in the kitchen and asked myself if all of those familiar objects would recognize my mother with her brand-new face.

Ten days later, she came back with the news that, in a month and a half, she was going to La Pampa with Sara. Someone at the Macachín City Hall had called my aunt to tell her they had found some boxes with their last name on them in a warehouse that was going to be demolished. If she wanted them, she would have to go get them in the next three months. After that, they would be getting rid of everything.

"Boxes? What's inside?"

"I don't know, they didn't say, but we both need to be there to sign some papers and get them. Sara was already planning on going for some business, so I'm going with her. It's only three days," she said while taking a painkiller. Then she added, almost in passing: "Julia is also coming. I asked her to join us."

What about me? Why was I never included? I opened my mouth to say something. I want... I want... She interrupted my thought before I could express it.

"I didn't want to bother you, that's why I didn't ask you. You have the baby on the way, and Antonio, and the renovation, and your job. Besides, you're not really interested in this, are you?"

Since Dad died, the idea of a trip to Macachín had crossed my mind a hundred times, but I didn't know how to go about it. Suddenly here it was, served to me on a silver platter, so I transformed my mother's question into an invitation that brought a smile to my face and left me floating in that perfect point in space, right before jumping off the swing.

"Yes. I want to go to the town where you were born," I replied.

After my accident, we never went back to Mar del Plata. When we stopped going, I understood what that house, which was sold a few years later, meant to me. The same happened with Dad. I don't want to learn what Mom means to me only once she is gone. A trip to La Pampa together could remedy that.

We arrive at Julia's. She is waiting for us downstairs, sitting in the hallway, clutching her designer purse. She walks to the car, tough as a precious stone. There's only a two-year age difference between us, but we don't really get along. She had twins at twenty and raised them on her own, becoming invisible to the rest of the world, like a pastel wallpaper in the background. For years her life consisted of playing with toy cars, swords, and soldiers, buying school supplies, and packing tighty-whities and sports shoes in gym bags. I don't know if she was happy; she was a mother. Now that the twins have flown the coop, she doesn't know what she is. She has the glassy gaze of a taxidermied animal.

I help her put her things in the trunk and we go pick up Sara, who is also waiting for us downstairs with her fiery red hair, all puffed up like cotton candy. She's a five-foot-ten breath of fresh air who speaks and lives restlessly. As soon as she sees us, she begins blowing kisses at us and walks toward the car in all her quirky clumsiness. She's wearing a leopard-print jacket and gold flats. The same outfit, for Miami or La Pampa.

We take the highway and Sara's story time begins.

"One of the first trips your mother and I took was to Piriápolis, in Uruguay, but the beach was too rocky, and we decided to keep going until Pelotas, in Brazil. When we got to the border, we had to take a detour along the coastline because the tide was low. It was a packed-sand road. The sea on one side, the dunes on the other. There we were, cool as cucumbers, until we noticed the water starting to rise when we still had a good way to go. Remember, sweetie?"

Mom nods. She likes hearing about herself from others.

"You know what I remember? The splash of the waves against our tires, it was crazy! We were crazy, Sarita."

Having Sara as an older sister allowed my mother to get away with never fully becoming an adult. She is still an irresponsible child. Family roles are indestructible.

We drive by a beat-up sign with the image of Our Lady of Luján, and Julia asks if we want to stop at the basilica. She wants to go in to check another item off her list. Last month she crossed the Andes on horseback. She's visiting Antarctica before the end of the year. She goes through the years as if at the supermarket, collecting anecdotes to fill her life's shopping cart.

"It's right there, let's go be tourists," she insists.

I park the car, and we enter the basilica in silence. None of us has seen its stunning adorned interior before, where angels float on delicate feet above the frigid air. Even though Mom is Jewish, Julia and I were baptized when we were born. Dad said he'd picked good godparents for the both of us, but he ended up growing apart from them and they stopped sending us birthday presents. My bond with the Catholic Church was acrimonious. After my first communion, I used to kneel by my bed, hands together at my chest, and pray to a bearded old man in a white tunic, sitting on a lonesome cloud against a pale blue background. My faith was simple. Maybe that's why it fell apart. Antonio went through something similar. He was five and we were on summer vacation at the beach when he told me he had seen Jesus going into the water. He had catechism class in school. The next day, he pointed to the shore and told me again, "Look, Mom, there's Jesus in the water!" I looked up and saw a skinny drunkard, half naked with a tattered pair of pants walking amidst the waves, holding a wine carton. His beard was biblical.

We walk around the clammy nave as if whispering, Mom holding onto Julia's arm. The outside murmur sounds like the ocean inside a seashell—only the noise of Sara's shoes disturb the quiet. To test the echo in one of the side arches, I utter my tongue twister. *Peter Piper picked a peck of pickled peppers, a peck of pickled peppers Peter Piper picked.* Mom looks at me like I'm a crazy person. I lean in and ask her what she makes of churches.

"I mean... these poor people. I despise religion."

"What about Judaism?"

"That's not a religion."

"What is it then?"

"A people... a feeling... Whatever else they might be, a Jew is first and foremost a Jew. Can't be explained. People who have to ask don't get it."

Mom thinks words are used to reduce reality to something the mind can process. That's why she hesitates. Words are not enough. Some labels, however, come in handy for her. She insists her people are the only three worthy minorities: the Jews, the homosexuals, and the Marxists (although I've never met a single Marxist friend of hers). "In order to survive, they had no other option but to rise above the rest," she explains. When I tell her the Roma are also a minority, she says "Well, not them," and changes the subject.

Inadvertently, we find ourselves by a group of foreigners. Julia gets closer to the tour guide to try to catch some interesting trivia. Mom grabs my arm and pulls me back.

"Let them pass, I don't like going first," she tells me.

"Me neither, I'm sheepish," I reply.

She gives me a surprised look and smiles at me conspiratorially, and next thing we know we are left behind, in silence except for the swooshing sound of our pants as we walk.

We come back to the car with a bag of tangerines and pastries from one of those touristy stands where you can get fried dough and rosaries, prayer cards, and carved mate cups.

Mom requests we put on some classical music. Years ago, she spent entire afternoons in the dark listening to opera. Now she keeps busy with modern art. Julia asks what she's in the mood for.

"*Rigoletto*," she answers, and both my sister and I know exactly what she'll say next: "It was your father's favorite opera. The part he liked the most was the heartbreaking cry in the last act: la maledizione!"

Mom misses Dad but doesn't say so. It's a verb she has sequestered, like when we were children in the car and were forbidden from asking how much longer. I would say, "I'm not asking how long, but I would like to know when we will arrive at our destination." Instead of conjugating the verb "to miss," Mom asks to listen to *Rigoletto*. She closes her eyes, rests her head back, and falls asleep.

Mom and Dad met in May 1977 in New York at a restaurant called The Cellar, which is still there, near the Flatiron, that building featured in every Big Apple guidebook, named for its resemblance to an iron. Soon after it was built in the early twentieth century, it became an attraction for perverts looking to catch a glimpse of skin, since the winds at the intersection used to lift dresses à la Marilyn Monroe in *The Seven Year Itch*. Dad had a crush on Marilyn, and that movie was his favorite. When he turned seventy, Mom gave him a framed poster of his blonde obsession, and he put it up over the bed in their weekend cottage.

There were four of them at The Cellar that night: Mom went with Sara and Dad with Lydia, his first wife, a very American woman who kept calling him at home until the day he died. For my mother and her sister, it was their first time in the United States, and someone had put them in touch with my father—who traveled to New York often—so he could show them around. He was already a successful financier, his pockets bulging with money he earned for himself and others. Once at the restaurant, my mother and father sat across the table from each other and ended up talking all night. She was wearing a gold lamé dress with shoulder pads that accentuated her thick hair the color of wet raven's feathers. It was a rental, and the sticky metallic fabric wasn't very comfortable, but she wanted to flirt with the world. To impress Dad, she told him about her trip to Russia, where she had been a year before with a group of doctors from the Hospital de Clínicas. She didn't think to mention that's where she had worked for eight years, doing her shift and taking over others' in various hospitals to be able to afford the rent for the studio apartment where she lived. Lydia and Sara talked about labels and designers. For dessert, Mom and Dad ordered strawberry flambé to share, and that was the beginning of her metamorphosis from rags to riches.

Before long the two met again in Buenos Aires at another restaurant, the Ligure—this time, alone. It was one of those typical restaurants in the city with bowtied waiters and a black leather menu of endless pages that had remained unchanged for over seven decades. He talked about whatever, and she stared at him as if hypnotized, without saying or eating anything until Dad explained to her how things were going to go down from then on: "Finish your meal," he told her. Mom, radiant, ate her artichoke quiche, the restaurant's specialty, which my father had ordered for her. He had calves' brains in black butter reduction. When they were on their way out, Dad got serious and told her he had a confession to make: "I'm Jewish," he said, stone-faced. He had an incomprehensible sense of humor, and someone else might have taken offense, but she just cackled and put him on a pedestal ever since. They were meant for each other.

Dad stayed with Lydia for a few more months after that. It wasn't easy to leave that green-eyed blonde with legs for days who walked as gracefully as a panther. So much so that even nowadays I still find letters from her in old forgotten drawers at home. I also found lists of women's names. Mom appears on top followed by thousands of phantom goddesses, a mysterious constellation of girls. As a teenager, I found his little doll collection disgusting, but now I see the name "Inés" and I imagine a pair of full lips, I read "Victoria" and I think of the body of a gazelle. Lydia is also featured in these lists, but her I always loathed. Blondes can really trigger a vicious hatred. Mom acknowledges that she was a difficult rival, with the laughter of a hyena. Every time she smiled, Lydia showed her fangs. Because she was American, she couldn't decipher the etiquette required to satisfy an Argentine macho, and this was the final straw that led my father to my mother: Lydia was not an obedient woman. Just two days after my dad asked her to leave the house, my mom came in as her replacement and quickly adapted to her new role as his wife. That same day she quit her job as a doctor and never went back to work again.

Her fascination with him was absolute ever since she first laid eyes on him. When Lucas, my partner, turned forty, he reminded Mom that that was how old my father had been when she met him. We all know The Cellar story; it's one we always hear at the table after a few drinks. Who can say they're free from repetition?

"Oh please, but there's no comparison," she said smiling and taking another bite of her cheesecake. Lucas wasn't offended. He didn't understand what she was telling him.

Mom always thought Dad was ugly, but that was trivial: "there is no such thing as an ugly man." What captivated her was being next to someone who occupied such a space in the world: a powerful, cultured, fun, self-sufficient man. By his side, she gave up on making a life for herself and began feeling totally at ease being someone's wife.

Mom shows off her fingers with diamond and ruby rings my father gifted her. She keeps her jewelry in a drawer, wrapped in little turquoise-blue velveteen bags. Sometimes I try them on, and she gets nervous. She doesn't like having certain things played with. She wears the gold ones to her card games, the sapphire one to go to the theatre, the emerald one for weddings. She would have loved having a wedding band, but Dad never complied. When they met, he was still married to Lydia and there was not yet a divorce law in Argentina. Once it passed, Dad couldn't be bothered to go back to city hall. I used to brag about my parents not being married, as if it made me edgy. But for Mom, it was like living in a mansion with no locks in the middle of a shady neighborhood. Six months after my father's death, and despite the fact that he was careful to sell the cottage beforehand and leave the inheritance in easy-to-administer bank accounts, Mom said the money was not enough and took the case to court. A judge recognized her as the deceased's wife and authorized her to earn a pension as his widow. Two acquaintances had to testify that they had been together for over three decades. One was Luis, Dad's driver. The other was Oscar, the super.

A few weeks ago, we found a folder full of letters and faxes my father had sent or received throughout his life. One said: "Elena, I arrive tonight. Flight AR 1120. Tell Luis to pick me up. We're going to the opera. Wear the black dress I bought you. I'm leaving for Paris on Saturday." All his correspondence is in the same style.

"I never knew what he thought of me," my mom told me one afternoon. We were sitting on her bedroom floor, our legs stretched out in a V shape and our backs against the closet door that never closed properly.

"And you of him?"

She shook her head, raised her eyebrows, and set her gaze on the carpet. She took a breath of stale air and said:

"I had a deep admiration for your father, but I don't think I was ever in love with him."

"Well, what does being in love mean to you?" I asked her, surprised.

"Something else. Something I felt for another man."

Then she stood up to go to the bathroom, wiping a tiny tear hanging from her eyelashes.

I am the only one awake in the car. I turn the music off and try to find something on the radio. I give up after hearing an intergalactic crackle in between stations. A drizzle starts to fall, light but incessant. On the side of the road, the wind bends the shrubland creating odd shapes. Soon, the rain is behind us, but a heavy fog forces me to slow down. Sara wakes up and asks where we are.

"Villa Fournier."

Julia, who's been fast asleep since the basilica, sits up, wipes the corner of her lips, and eyes still sleepy, asks if this is where it happened.

"Where what happened?" I reply.

"The accident."

"See that curve by the hill? It was right there," says Sara, and it's story time again.

In the home of my grandparents Abraham and Natalia, where Sara and Mom lived, conversation was always pure business talk. Not about stocks and bonds, but about the town's business: who bought and sold what, how someone became rich, or how someone else lost everything.

Mom wakes up, amused by the word, which she has forgotten all about.

"Business!" she repeats and laughs out loud in a way I've never heard before.

Immediately, I understand this word is at the core of their family. As kids, they'd heard it time and again from their father, their uncles, their grandparents. After dinner, the house was filled with relatives talking business. In those eight letters, Sara and Mom meet, see one another, and resurrect a world no longer there.

I ask them about their family lexicon, and they both yell in unison:

"Koldre!"

It means—I find out—"quilt" in Yiddish. It was one of those words that got mixed in with Spanish in their household.

"It was only as an adult that I learned it was in another language. As a kid, quilt was koldre," explains Mom.

Sara nods. Their childhood is marked by those words that belong only to them. But it was "business" that shaped them so differently since my aunt took to it from a young age, and Mom, never. My grandfather had a dry goods store he had inherited from his brother, Uncle Isaac, the only one in the family with true business savvy.

"Dad also had a grain warehouse, a salt lake, and more. There was a reason people called me a 'millionaire' in school," says Sara. She speaks gracefully, a woman untouched by bitterness.

When Mom and Sara were still fighting over dolls, business started going south and my grandfather got caught in a vortex of depression. He sat at the kitchen table and proceeded to remove from his pocket the crumpled papers on which he wrote down his mounting debts. Sara, at twelve restless years old, gathered and straightened the papers, then did the math to try to figure out how to pay back the creditors. Mom was still too young, and when she finally grew old enough to understand, she refused to learn the meaning of any word connected to the world of accounting, all while Sara fell in love with balance sheets.

"I could never forgive him. Could never justify his failure, his attitude," Mom says quietly, as such things should be uttered. "He gave up instead of being a man."

Her anger is not enough to make her hate her father as she might have wanted; she just feels embarrassed by him. Her shame sits heavy on her breastbone because she must have really loved him. The shame of a child for a father is devastating; it can disarm you, render you powerless. If my grandfather had been a lovable fool, the type of imprudent and impulsive man who can get away with making mistakes, maybe my mother would have known how to raise us, and Sara would have gotten married. But he had to be prudent, an ordinary fearful man. I have deep empathy for Abraham. Or maybe it's compassion. At the time of his death, he had spent years doing nothing, just lying in bed, being taken care of by my grandmother. There was nothing wrong with him; he was just consumed by sadness, by failure. He weighed a hundred pounds. Sara says he received insulin shock treatments in Buenos Aires.

"What is that?" I ask.

"You know those infamous electric shocks? Like that, but worse," answers Mom.

"And the accident they died in, what happened?" asks Julia, at the same time the thought pops into my head. Some questions just have to come up all at once.

Sara says it was after one of those medical trips (when my grandfather was fifty-seven and my grandmother fifty) that an elderly man named Pipkin offered them a ride back to La Pampa. Abraham was sitting in the front next to Pipkin, and Natalia was in the back. Pipkin was closely tailgating a truck, and when he tried to pass, he crashed into an oncoming car.

"All three of them were killed. Everyone in the other car was fine. Pipkin and Dad died instantly. Mom, we were told, put up a bit of a fight. The car looked like an accordion; I saw it. The engine wound up in the front seat."

"That's right," says Mom.

Someone called their place in Buenos Aires to let them know their parents had been in an accident. Mom picked up; she was sixteen. She had stayed home because she had the flu. She doesn't remember if the caller said her parents were dead or if they only told her about the accident. Mom called her uncles who were with Sara in the Quilmes country house, and they took off immediately. Sara thinks she didn't know they were dead because when they arrived in Villa Fournier, she couldn't understand why they were wasting so much time at the police station instead of rushing to the hospital.

"'Let's go to the hospital,' I told them, 'come on, let's go.' But we never went."

I always thought that the day my mother and aunt opened up about the death of their parents they'd break down in tears, but they seem unfazed. After so many years, maybe they've gotten used to it and are now numb. Or maybe my grandparents stopped protecting them long before their deaths. It was then my mother got cozy underneath Sara's long arms, as if nestling under the wings of a stork. But the wings of a sibling are nothing like those of a parent.

The road reappears before my eyes. The fog lifts, and so does our intimacy. Then Mom says Abraham had crystal clear eyes, so translucently blue they looked almost diabolic. I have never seen a single picture of him. I don't know what he looked like or what I've inherited from him, but I can't wait for nightfall so I can lie on the open grass and feel the starry acupuncture on my skin.

We break for lunch at a parrilla in Trenque Lauquen after a recommendation from a local wearing a mustache and a neckerchief who we met when we stopped for gas. The tables, the chairs, and the glasses are plastic. So is the breadbasket. They bring out a seltzer siphon and a strip of gristle and bone with fries.

While Julia shakes her blouse to clear out the crumbs, Sara responds to my interrogation. We play a ping-pong match of keen questions and incomplete answers to close the distance between us. We barely know each other. My family is not too familiar.

"What games did you play growing up?" I ask.

"We biked around town."

"What was your grandfather like?"

"My zeyde was called León. He had a long beard and spent his days reading the Torah."

"He was a bum," Mom interjects.

"What was your best friend's name?"

"Ruth. She was great."

"During the polio epidemic she was paralyzed with fear, and a rumor went around town that she had contracted it. Remember, Sarita?" asks Mom.

Sara doesn't remember.

"And what did you do on weekends?"

"We went to the movies, which played non-stop films on Saturdays. We would go in at two in the afternoon and come out at nine at night."

"What else do you remember?"

Mom takes the lead.

"I remember the day a businessman came by for dinner and told us about a revolution in Cuba. He said in ten years all of Latin America would be communist."

Sara chuckles. She makes fun of the businessman, of Fidel Castro, of Mom. My grandmother Natalia said no to everything, and she blames her for that cowardice. When Sara left home to go live on her own in Buenos Aires while finishing up her studies and attending law school, my grandfather used to send her a wagonload of salt that she sold to a grain warehouse. That money was enough to last her—and later my mother and her—one or two months. Salt was all Abraham had left and it was what supported Sara and Mom after their parents died in the accident. Once, the buyer told my aunt he didn't need her salt because he had enough, and when the wagon arrived, she didn't have room to store it. The transport company gave her a twelve-hour deadline for unloading the salt, otherwise she'd lose it. In a frenzy, she walked all around Avellaneda for hours until she finally found a leather tanning company and convinced the owner to purchase the entire order. She was eighteen years old. Over the course of the next fifty-eight, my aunt grew rich off salt.

Mom doesn't like talking about that. Sara immediately notices her sister's discomfort. She mimics her signature in the air, asking the waiter for the check. Then she tells us:

"You know what I remember? The white gloves I wore to see the train pass by. Have I told you they called me the 'millionaire'?"

Before hitting the road again, I go out to stretch my legs and call Lucas. He's with Antonio at the new place. I picture them at the construction site, walking among rubble and exposed beams, wrecked by time. I'm glad I'm not there.

We moved into Mom's with only our clothes and Antonio's toys. The rest of our stuff we stored all in a single room at the new house in piled-up boxes and under an old sheet now covered in suffocating dust. It weighs on me like another belly that, day after day, grows not bigger but lopsided: the boxes on top crush the ones below, and the cardboard collapses like an accordion. I don't even want to think about my wine glasses or my dishes—brittle, cracking overnight without anyone hearing it. Every time I stop by, I lift that ghostly skirt as if identifying a corpse to confirm that yes, my life is still there, stored in cardboard boxes.

My way of handling problems is by tidying up rooms and organizing closets, so I tend to avoid going by the construction site. The work is progressing infinitely slower than my galloping anxiety imagining our future home. Once the staircase is finally ready, I think about when the flagstone entryway will be done; when I see that the windowsills have been sanded, I obsess over the kitchen counters. At twenty-eight weeks pregnant, I start fantasizing about when the baby will walk. Lucas, conversely, likes playing contractor, straddling the beams that at some point will support the flooring. He's in charge of requesting backsplash estimates, choosing the wood slats, discussing structural issues with the architect. Better this way; I don't need to know what a double T beam is, or the difference between a tied and a composite column. I don't need to be making important decisions. I can only think of drawer pulls and light switches, which I hope can be vintage, you know, those old stiff ones.

The first time we saw the house before buying it, we left upset. Floor to ceiling, it was crammed with heavy furniture, with depressing crocheted doilies covering the dining table and every other surface. You could barely walk without bumping into something. The sunlight turned sepia as it filtered through the stained-glass windows. My guess was the owner probably smelled of mothballs. But the asking price was so low that we decided to go back with Ezequiel, our architect, to see what could be done. That second time, we were greeted by Valery, the eighty-year-old owner. She was wearing rouge, a stifling ash-blue dress, and a pair of clunky black shoes that made her look like a spinster. She wasn't. She had lived there for fifty-seven years with her husband and their three children, and she wanted a young family to move into the house. You could tell she was a healthy woman, capable of bearing impossible pains with dignity, like the death of her son a few months ago. That was the reason for selling. "Too many memories. Sometimes it's best to put them to rest," she told us. She didn't sound like an old lady. She had the voice of a femme fatale, and it was that strength in her vocal cords that won us over. I wasn't sold on the idea of living in a place so loaded with someone else's history, but we closed two weeks later.

Antonio also loves wandering around the rubble at the construction site. He plays with pieces of abandoned bricks he finds in one of the downstairs bedrooms, now serving as both a storeroom and a garbage dump. He builds volcanos and towers with whatever he finds in there. He wants me to play with him, but I'm never up for it. It's rare for two people to ever want the same thing at the same time. Antonio is not like those spoiled kids who think they're the center of the universe. But I'm also not a cool mom. When he was born, his shrieks pierced my stomach. No one had warned me about the brutal selfishness of babies. And while I loved his newborn smell and soft skin, surrendering to him didn't come naturally. I stayed as far as possible from baby talk, using language designed for keeping my distance. It was my way of working through my anger. A friend of mine who worked at a hospital in Brazil told me she saw dozens of cases of shaken baby syndrome. Desperate mothers who shook their kids to quiet them, sometimes for only two or three seconds. But even then, the bleeding it caused inside their babies' little heads was irreversible. They'd arrive at the ER all blue. Antonio hadn't been born yet, and back then I had no idea what she was talking about. Afterward, I understood. I learned that love is so close to cruelty that you must stay alert to avoid crossing the line. Becoming a mother was painful. Even now, several times a day, I just have to stop, sit, put my head down. I get so tired.

"How's the trip? Are you in Santa Rosa yet? I'm about to decide on the light fixtures and water heater. Did you give it some thought? Anything I should mention to Ezequiel when he comes by?" Lucas asks loudly, excitedly. He's like a plane taking off, full of force and speed. I was crazy about his energy when we met, going skinny-dipping and making out under the water. Once upon a time, we were like that, content. Now he drains me. I wish he'd turn off his engine.

"All good, we're still a ways from Santa Rosa. We just had lunch in Trenque Lauquen. Can you put Antonio on so I can say hello?"

I exit the restaurant in search of better reception, and the cold air makes my teeth chatter. Antonio tells me he's building one of his volcanos. His voice sounds sweeter over the phone, like chamomile. When it's my turn to look after him, sometimes I feed him junk food. I put on the TV and give him chocolates. Lucas spends less time with him, but they play together like a puppy with a tennis ball. They are friends.

"Dad says he'll help me build a fire inside the volcano so we can make it erupt! I have to go find some paper, bye-bye, I'll put Dad back on!"

He cuts me off before I can say not to and Lucas is now telling me that when I get back I should go look at carpeting for our bedroom. I don't trust carpeted floors, but I'd rather not bring it up. I'll have a comfy room that can absorb hairs and nail clippings; body parts fallen from grace. If I wasn't so wishy-washy, I'd tell Ezequiel to redesign the place to have two main bedrooms, as if we were royalty. Couples put up with a lot out of fear of offending each other. Separate bedrooms and bathrooms, that'd be a healthy start.

"I'll call you tonight," I tell him as I see my mother leaving the restaurant and getting into the car. I follow her and get in the driver's seat.

"What about the others?" I ask her.

"In the bathroom. They're coming. Who was that on the phone?"

"Lucas. He's at the new place."

Mom and Lucas get along. They understand each other better than they understand me. Maybe that's because they don't expect anything from each other.

"And? How's that going? Quite the renovation you're doing."

"Yeah, it's a lot. But it's either now or never," I tell her, turning on the car to get some heat.

"I'm convinced that the less you do, the better. As soon as you start fixing one thing, something else breaks. It's the same with people," she preaches.

Mom is such a coward. At times, she can be pretty inappropriate too. I used to be so embarrassed by her as a kid. *Are you Jewish? Who's the wife? Would you give me a discount if I pay in cash?* I would tug at her hand and mumble: *Mommm...*

"I feel so huge, I can't imagine how I'll make it through the third trimester," I say, adjusting the seat to my comfort.

This belly grows, and my skeleton makes room for it. Hips open up, ribs move outward, looking for air. Only I notice these changes, my body searching for a new balance.

"Yeah, you're a lot bigger than with Antonio."

"What if I give birth to a monster!"

"All pregnant women obsess over deformities, don't worry about it."

Once, after seeing an exhibit by an American photographer, Mom talked to me about giants, albinos, and Siamese twins. According to her, circus freaks had an advantage: they were born broken. For the rest of us, it is life that breaks us.

"How comforting. I feel much better now, thanks," I reply. Mom cackles. I smile.

Soon after Dad died, I wished I could go back to being a kid and cuddle in Mom's arms. I needed to feel safe. But she never noticed. Inside, she's an origami figure. She folds into herself.

I'd like to think we've grown closer now.

Julia comes out. She signals for me to lower my window and says she wants to drive from Trenque Lauquen to Santa Rosa, so I move over to the backseat and fall asleep in an uncomfortable semi-fetal position with my head against the door. Before long, I wake up in pain. It's my back. It's been years since I last felt that pinch, and I panic. I try not to think about the word "dorsal" while I move carefully, more aware than ever of my own fragility. The burning sensation crawls up my spine and makes me shudder. I count to myself. I breathe in and out. I count again. Numbers are like a red light; they make it stop.

"Are you OK?" my mom asks, sitting beside me.

"It's my back."

"Ah, the back," she says looking down and stroking her dry hands. She shrugs it off. The silence between us is always an interruption.

Again, I feel a stabbing pain down my back, and it's like I'm eleven all over. My mom never mentioned the accident again, she hastily packed it away in a moldy corner. She only spoke about it when I asked her, before marrying Lucas, if I could have children.

"I don't know. You were so young when it happened, I didn't think to ask the doctor about it," was her brief answer.

"But do you think that if I ever want kids I'll be able to have a normal pregnancy?"

I don't remember what she said, she was in a hurry, had to go run some errands, buy butter, cheese, whatever.

Despite my fears, when I got pregnant with Antonio, I was able to handle the pregnancy and delivery without any complications. The accident only left sporadic flashes of pain, like today, and the inability to sleep on my stomach. I sleep on my side with a pillow between my legs. The physical side effects are easy to name. The others, left unspoken, crowd around my vertebrae. What was my mother looking at the day I fell?

"I'm going to try and sleep it off," I tell her.

"Yes, good idea, Ema. Just rest up."

When we arrive at the hotel, I wake up with my mind numb and my face creased, but without pain. We get out of the car and my sister suggests going to the casino. My mother agrees. She believes in chance.

"Let's meet in the lobby in an hour, so we have time to take a shower and relax a bit," Sara says.

She's sharing a room with Mom. Julia and I stay in another, like when we were growing up. It's the best thing we ever shared—maybe the only thing. Relationships between sisters are a mystery. Sara and Mom couldn't live without each other, yet Julia and I never even miss each other.

As kids, we used to play with a makeup set that Dad brought us from one of his trips to Europe. I played the client. I sat on the toilet seat with my eyes closed, and Julia did my makeup, tickling my eyelids and lips. Don't open your eyes, she said, wait until I'm finished. Although she made no effort to hide her laughter, when I peeked into the mirror I thought I looked beautiful. I didn't care that it was too much blush.

At school, I worshipped her. She materialized every time a girl with tight braids called Laurita Aguirre was about to make me the target of her bullying. As soon as Laurita saw Julia, she chickened out and went looking for another victim without an older sister. I could suddenly breathe again and was no longer in danger of peeing my pants. Laurita really had it in for me, but my sister was my savior. She didn't even have to say anything; all it took was for her to come over with her friends or give me a nod of recognition. After school, she camped out in the kitchen and made study guides full of highlighted arrows that she later photocopied and sold to her classmates for a small fee. She decorated her original copy with glitter and filled the margins with notes in different colors: *cool!!!* and *yes!!!* and *wow!!!* in English. I've never seen anything like that since. On weekends, she teased her hair and wore it down, and she packed her arm with bangles that accentuated her slim wrists. She had a yellow Walkman and listened to mixtapes she got from the owner of a tattoo parlor. She told him she would get a rose behind her ear, a dolphin on her ankle, the word *LOVE* on the back of her neck. She spent hours sitting on a well-worn brown leather chair looking at designs in a binder. She would let me come with her under the one condition of not opening my mouth. She never actually got any tattoos though. She liked to tilt her head while speaking, stretching out her neck like a proud orchid. Yet it wasn't her posture that inspired my respect, but the fact that she was two years older—a world of difference at that age.

As we grew, that gap narrowed, and soon enough, as we experimented with cheap hair dye on our heads and purple drinks at bars, Julia got pregnant. She had just turned twenty. She came home straight from the hospital and settled into our room with her two cribs and all her baby stuff. As for me, I had to move to the study.

Everything became a deadly threat to my sister: the balcony, the stove, the weather. Also honey, strawberries, tomatoes. All these disasters-in-waiting trapped her and exhausted us. Her motherhood made me queasy. It exuded a sickening smell of sour milk that still makes me gag. The one time Julia asked me to look after her kids while she went out for diapers, they both started crying as soon as the door closed behind her. I tried getting them milk drunk, but it didn't work. When my sister came back, they were covered in snot, their eyes all swollen and red.

"You're useless," she said.

"Their father is useless," I replied.

It was the only time I dared mention my faceless brother-in-law. She never said who he was, and I never asked. I said it on purpose, to hurt her, but she didn't fall for it. She was holding one baby on her hip and cleaning the other's face with her free hand. She didn't have time for me.

A year later, Julia finally moved into a condo in Belgrano that our father bought for her. That's where she raised her twins on all the candy they wanted. Once, I found myself by chance outside of my nephews' school, and I couldn't make her out in the crowd of mothers waiting for their kids. She wore the costume well: shapeless dresses and ugly necklaces. Motherhood swallowed her whole. There was nothing left of the happy and exciting person she was supposed to be.

Last year, the twins finished high school and got an apartment together. Julia became one of those toothless old lionesses at the zoo who refuse to leave their cage because they've lost their sense of purpose. She leads a life of clenched teeth and fake smiles.

The last time we bonded was when Dad got sick. Our family home became a medical facility that operated under the motto "keep calm and doctor on." We consulted specialists, filled prescriptions, reviewed test results, and coordinated ambulance transfers. Meanwhile, Dad's nose became sharper by the day, his eyes turned darker, more sunken, his arms skinnier. Julia and I took turns taking care of him each week. We communicated without talking as we swapped claims, bills, and prescriptions to avoid burdening Mom with paperwork. One night, Julia told me Dad was seeing hairy insects on the ceiling. She shared this with me during a hand-off early one morning as the sun was coming out. Then she started crying and hid her face in a threadbare, almost non-existent handkerchief. It was the only time I ever saw her choke up, but I couldn't bring myself to really comfort her. I just stroked her hair and then looked at my fingers, puzzled by that unfamiliar texture. She suggested we finish a list she'd started hours ago with Dad: female names starting with O. Odile Olga Oriana Olivia Olinda Ophelia Olympia Odette Odelia Ona. Dad liked to make absurd lists on scraps of paper we later found around the house. Asian capital cities, years and places where he spent his birthday, tangos by Gardel, Roman emperors. I couldn't think of any name with O, and after a while Julia put the list away without saying anything. This family enterprise lasted the nine months it took Dad to die. After that, we went back to being broken once more. We spoke without really saying anything, like those couples who kiss without tongue.

Before leaving for the casino, I lie belly-up on the bed and call Lucas again. I ask for Antonio, who tells me they baked a cake.

"It was so yummy! Dad got his T-shirt and pants all dirty!"

Listening to Antonio on the phone softens me. The day he was born, he came out looking so much like Lucas that one of his friends refused to hold him because the resemblance freaked him out. Since then, Lucas looks at our son like a bladesmith contemplating his own reflection in the glint of his knife. He's never looked at me with such enchantment. Not even on our wedding day, when I walked down the aisle appearing as perplexed as the day of my first communion. On the recording, my face is equal parts happy and shocked. Lucas does not appear in the frame.

"And what are you doing next?" I ask Antonio.

"Eating more cake!" he screams into my ear.

If we ever get separated, Lucas should keep him. He's the type of father who throws his child into the air, makes candy appear from his ear, and shares an entire bucket of popcorn. When Antonio has nightmares, it's Lucas he wants. I'm a light sleeper and can hear him come into our bedroom. I lie still and pretend to be asleep, but he walks past my side of the bed without even looking at me. Lucas wakes up, offers him some water, and takes him back to his bed. Sometimes Lucas doesn't come back. He falls asleep in Antonio's room, lying on the floor like a toy soldier, using his son's stuffed whale as a pillow.

"Do you want to talk to Dad?"

"No, it's all right, go eat your cake," I say. But Antonio puts him on anyway.

Lucas asks me about our hotel in Santa Rosa and what we're doing for dinner. The type of questions people ask while looking right at you, but with their minds elsewhere. Chicken or pasta, it doesn't matter. I ask him about his bar. He tells me about a new artisanal beer they're trying out. I immediately stop listening, thinking of something else while he talks on and on. At some point in our life together, Lucas went from being one of those catchy songs you want to listen to over and over again to one of those you just have to turn off so you don't lose your mind. That's the thing about listening to music on repeat. You grow weary of the loop.

While I'm still on the phone, Julia steps out of the bathroom and straightens her dress with her hands. She looks at herself in the mirror. She is sinewy, her hair is set. Just like she looks in photographs. I have no intention of changing my clothes, so I stay in bed. Being pregnant is the perfect excuse to let myself go; my belly is like a shield, my hair grows wild. She would never go out like this.

Before hanging up, I ask Lucas to give Antonio a kiss for me. I send another one just for him. They're interchangeable. Our relationship has turned into an abandoned campsite I can never make up my mind about leaving.

All three of us went to my most recent ultrasound appointment. While we were waiting to be called in, Antonio swung his legs impatiently in a room decorated with dying ferns and framed Renoir posters.

"I like three names: Juan, or Santi, or Moishe," he said.

"Moishe?" I inquired.

"Yes, that's what we call the redhead at school."

I didn't know he had a Jewish classmate.

"What if it's a girl? What names do you like? Alejandra, Sofía, Juvencia?"

Antonio frowned. He hadn't thought of any girl names.

During the ultrasound, the technician translated the blurry black-and-white images on the screen for us. Every few seconds, he said everything looked good. He kept adding gel and spreading it on my belly. The baby, he said, weighed almost sixteen ounces. A whole ribeye steak cooking inside me.

"Everything looks good," said the technician again. He had a receding hairline, a thick neck, and an amorphous body. I found him off-putting, but I tried thinking good thoughts to avoid interfering with the test results. I was trying to be good.

He then asked us if we wanted to know the sex. We nodded.

"It's a girl, see?" he said smiling, showing his tiny teeth, while pointing to a vague circle on the screen.

Antonio burst into uncontrollable tears that turned his face red in a matter of seconds. He covered his face with his hands and retreated into himself. Lucas gave him a hug and tried cracking some jokes. But Antonio wasn't laughing. I just thanked the technician.

On the way back, we got some ice cream. I had a pint of chocolate in honor of my daughter. Antonio ate his lemon cone in silence while Lucas kept trying to cheer him up. Then he said he had to run because one of his suppliers was waiting for him at the brewery.

Once at home, Antonio locked himself in his room to play with one of the puzzles I had designed for him the year before. It's a whale split up into forty-two pieces.

I let him be and went to my room, where I lifted my shirt and rubbed my belly. It was still sticky from the gel, and so stretched out it was beginning to look translucent. Two purplish veins ran up and down the circumference. My navel had popped, and it grossed me out. It's the only part of me that feels foreign, a black hole at the center of my body. I've never been able to keep it clean. I took my shirt off and turned to look at my new, incomprehensible shape in the mirror. Full breasts, hunched back, good-for-nothing belly, still not big enough to skip the line at the supermarket or get a seat on the bus. I stood up straight and the image improved. Slightly. I took off my pants and faced the mirror. I tilted my head in search of a new angle but couldn't find it. It's here, in this timid body, where everything happens. I got dressed again and went looking for Mom, who was on the phone in the kitchen, her refuge from the world. As soon as she saw me, she hung up and sat down in front of a plate full of leftovers.

"How's things?"

"I'm fat," I replied.

"Come on, you're pregnant. You need to gain weight. It's not like you're steatopygic."

Mom loves to sneak in big words and wait for you to ask about them. But I already knew "steatopygic." It refers to pear-shaped people. She had once told me herself, while we were watching a film. An actress with a tiny frame got out of the pool with an ass like a rhinoceros.

"It's a girl," I told her, my hands on my belly.

"You're kidding! I could have sworn you were having another boy!"

"Antonio started crying when he found out."
She laughed.
"You put ideas in his head."
"I didn't put anything in his head."
"Of course you did, all the time. It's inevitable. We spoil them. Domesticate them."

Mom also likes dramatic phrases. "Nothing is certain, except misfortune, but it should come already and get it over with!" she repeats like a mantra. She goes through her days stoically. Sometimes she may seem content, but she lives a shrunken existence. If she has to go out to dinner or buy some milk, she wears shoulder pads. Her coats, blouses, and T-shirts all have beige shoulder pads that offer her more of a structure to endure her life. That's her style: a year-round, several-decades-old trend that never goes out of fashion.

I sat down with her and wished she'd talk to me more, open up at least once so I could know what she thinks, what she feels. It's really upsetting to live with a mother who never lets her guard down. What she offers me doesn't cut it, it's not enough. But what is most disappointing is that she doesn't ask for anything from me—to know she doesn't need me.

"Where's Antonio?" she asked from her corner.
"He's playing."
"And Lucas?"
"At the brewery."

Mom dabbed at the crumbs on her plate before putting them in her mouth. Then she moved her head ever so slightly and tossed her hair back.

"Well, I'm taking off. I have quite the day ahead of me."

I sat there, my fingers intertwined on my belly, trying not to think. Then I felt a kick from inside.

The Santa Rosa casino only has slot machines, metal monstrosities that wolf down people who wear too much makeup, dress in golden tights, and have dentures. The main room is almost empty, only seven couples as far as I can tell, their eyes lost on the screens in front of them. *Lemon, lemon, cherry. Cherry, BAR, cherry. Lemon, BAR, 7.* A friend from college got hired once to design slot machine seating. She was specifically asked to use a non-absorbent material since many players would rather soil themselves than leave their spot. The casino needed something easy to clean. She suggested upholstering the seats with diapers. I remember this story and walk slowly among the machines in search of leaks and suspicious stains.

We go to the bar and sit at a round table, too small for four strangers. We order a bottle of champagne and two ham-and-cheese paninis.

The bubbly is quick to make them tipsy. We share ridiculous stories.

"My friends are all seeing someone," says Mom. "Sonia is dating this man she's known since she was a teenager, so they have nothing to talk about. They've known each other their whole lives, imagine that."

"And what about your suitors?" asks Julia.

I didn't even know Mom had suitors. She never tells me anything.

"They're the worst. I went out with one who wouldn't shut up about his brilliant children and grandchildren. What do I care?! It would never cross my mind to tell him about the twins or Antonio."

Mom doesn't know our kids nor does she care to. She doesn't even pretend to be their grandmother. As she says that, she giggles nervously, a mix of cheeky embarrassment and brutal honesty.

"They're not like Juanma, he was great," she continues.

"Excuse me? Juanma?!" I yell over the loud eighties' music taking over the room.

Calling him Juanma demonstrates an intimacy that surprises me. Nicknames reconfigure people, redefine them. Mother is different from mom or mommy, Juan María is different from Juanma. At home years ago, I found a Spanish dictionary that I still have. On the first page, in the upper right corner, there was a stamp with the name *Juan María Álzaga*. All I know is that he was her big love before Dad. I didn't know she called him Juanma.

"She never told you about Juanma?" Julia asks me, acting all superior. She loves to be in the know, one step ahead.

"Sure, but I didn't know she called him that," I answer, defensively.

Mom lets herself be carried away by the champagne. She talks and every word becomes a sparkle. Juanma, I find out, was a married man when they met. He was ugly (like all the men she finds attractive), several years older, and a tenured professor at the university where she was a student. After class, he took her to the most expensive restaurants in Buenos Aires because he was "very fancy." Mom reminisces about the Italian restaurant downtown where they used to go and about the pasta arrabiata she always ordered.

"Not too long ago," she confesses, "I went all the way there and asked the police officer standing on that corner if he knew the restaurant. He took off his cap and scratched his head. It looked like he was thinking about it, but really he was just fighting the heat. He told me no, he didn't know any eating places around. He lowered his eyes and continued scrolling on his phone."

I find it sweet, picturing her talking to the police officer, trying to recover something that no longer exists. I'd sometimes like to press rewind, too. It was Mom, after all, who taught me the meaning of the word "elegy."

She says that after Dad died, she looked up Juan María online, but she only found a website accusing him of medical malpractice.

"When I called the Hospital Argerich, where he used to be the head of dermatology, I was told they didn't know him. Poor Juanma," she adds with a pitying expression on her face.

While the waiter brings another bottle, I grab my phone and search for Juan María on Facebook.

"Here you go," I tell her, pointing to his office phone number on the screen. There's no harm in dreaming at this point in her life. Mom takes out pen and paper from her purse and writes the number down with that illegible handwriting of hers that I abhor. Doctors are said to have poor penmanship due to the affliction of excessive handwriting: they're in school for over a decade and then spend their lives scribbling the same prescriptions; mantras ending in *zole/ine/one*. The same happens with people's signatures, they get stretched out, deformed, ruined. They change without permission. The same happens with almost everything, but some things are more visible than others.

Sara, who has been listening in silence while gobbling up her panini, interjects:

"Sweetie, the love of your life was Eduardo, not Juanma."

She finishes her drink and orders sparkling water.

Eduardo? I glance at Julia and see she's just as lost as me, but she doesn't say anything. She doesn't know who Sara is talking about either. I'm bubbling over with excitement. Learning about Mom's past feels like the first snow day of the season. I want to run down the stairs, open the door, jump around, and make snow angels until I'm out of breath.

Apparently, Eduardo was also married and ugly. And another of Mom's teachers—this time, of piano. They used to listen to Mozart's clarinet concerto together. He came from a family of celebrated pianists that were immortalized in a cult documentary. He barely made an appearance in the film's eighty-seven minutes. The bravura belonged to his wife, his daughter, and his granddaughter, whose fingers moved across the ivory keys with a passion as enviable as it was eerie. Julia googles Eduardo on her phone and several articles pop up with photos of him with his daughter. Mom doesn't look at the pictures. She's seen them already. She's looked him up several times before. At seventy-three years old, she's addicted to the internet. She says it's more dangerous than surfing at high tide. She takes computer lessons from a man who has a cosmic patience and access to all her passwords. Sometimes she asks him to download an app for playing bridge. Other times, she asks him to fix the air conditioner.

"Let me see," Sara says, putting on her glasses. "He looks exactly the same! But my goodness, his daughter looks so matronly. When your mother took piano lessons, she was crawling on the floor and eating dust bunnies. Look at her now!"

"Let me remind you that she's a world-famous musician now," Mom says.

Julia looks lost still. She chews on her panini slowly and covers her champagne glass with her hand to prevent a refill.

"Have you ever thought about what your life would have looked like if you'd stayed together?" I ask.

No answer.

"Have you?" I repeat.

Silence fills the long pause. That's the end of it. Mom is that unreachable stretch of skin between my shoulder blades, the one itchy inch I can't scratch.

Soon after Dad's death, Mom asked me to go with her to the Adventist Medical Center in Entre Ríos. She needed to detox. Julia couldn't make it and Mom didn't want to postpone it because the off-season was ending soon, as were the promotional rates. It was a tiresome trip, but I needed to be close to her, so I accepted the invitation, and the following Friday we set out for four days in Puiggari.

Mom goes every year. After her stay, and for a few weeks, she cuts out coffee, cigarettes, alcohol, and sugar. She goes to bed early and wakes up early. She walks. Then she falls off the wagon and relapses into life.

I drove nonstop for four hours through hills and weeping willows, and we arrived just before sunset. The place was a white two-story building that looked like a nursing home with pots of impatiens out front. The entry hall was decorated with eight colorful posters featuring natural remedies: water, rest, exercise, sunlight, fresh air, balanced nutrition, temperance, and faith in God. Before coming, Mom learned that Adventists believe in salvation. Also in discipline, the second coming of Christ, the new Earth. And in Saturday as the day of rest. I liked this Sabbath thing.

In the lobby, there was a man complaining. He wanted a diet without restrictions. He didn't come to lose weight but the opposite, he actually needed to gain some. He had a slightly grating voice and kept drumming his fingers on the counter.

"The doctor will make that call tomorrow," the receptionist told him and then turned to us: "Welcome, and you are…?"

She gave us two forms to complete. One with personal information, the other with forty questions including:

How often do you...

 ...think something is wrong with you?
 ...feel like hiding under the covers?
 ...feel bothered by criticism?
 ...have trouble sleeping?

Sitting on a white pleather chair, Mom checked forty boxes under the "very often" column. I stuck to "sometimes," right in the middle, and then divided the rest of my checkmarks evenly on both sides.

A young man showed us to our room upstairs. We rode the elevator with a huge man in a robe. He was all sweaty and could barely breathe. Every time he inhaled, his nose let out a labored whistle. His face was red. Mom looked at him.

"Excuse me..."

Mommm...

"...how much do you weigh?"

I looked down.

"A lot," he replied.

We went into our room. There was a towel swan and a little bar of hotel soap on each bed. On the night table, the Holy Scriptures. The curtains were an orange color, the synthetic wood floor was clean, and the bathroom had brown tile.

"These are your schedules for tomorrow," said the young man, handing us some brochures. "Dinner is downstairs in half an hour," he added before leaving without a tip.

I sat at the edge of the bed and petted the swan's coarse beak.

"What did I tell you? Looks straight out of Eastern Europe," Mom said.

I opened my brochure. It said I was placed in the resting group. I could eat and do as I pleased. As usual, Mom was in the chronic stress group, and on a 900-calorie diet.

"What's the difference? Nothing here tastes good anyway," she said.

I sneezed and it felt like my head was splitting. I was tired from the drive. And all those questions. *How often do you wish you could turn off your mind? Do you wish you could turn off your mind? Do you wish you could turn off your mind?*

After dinner, I lay in bed. Mom went around the room turning on the lights, making noise, looking for stuff. I realized I'd never shared a room with her before. We lived in the same house, yes, but sharing a room is much more intimate, and there is no intimacy between my mother and me. Pulling a Houdini trick, I took off my bra inside my T-shirt, and when she wasn't looking, I changed quickly out of the T-shirt and into my nightgown.

The following morning, they woke us up at six for a walk. Breakfast was at seven-thirty. Then there were lectures and massage sessions. Lunch was at noon. There was an aqua aerobics class at two, a healthy-eating workshop at three-thirty, high tea at four-thirty, sauna and hot tub at six, and another lecture at seven-thirty. Dinner was at eight.

"There, let's sit over there, next to the ambassador," Mom said pointing to a table in the back where a man was having soup.

"How do you know he's an ambassador?"

"I recognized his last name. He was at the chronic stress lecture. He must be retired by now."

We walked over there with our trays and sat across the table from the man. In a low voice, Mom asked him if he had been an ambassador. Yes. It was him. He had lived in West and East Germany, the United States, and Italy. He spoke five languages. He was a learned man. Mom was spellbound. They talked about a mutual friend of Dad's while I half-heartedly stirred the remains of a thick broth, no added salt. He told us that since his retirement he kept busy with genealogy. He was making his family tree. He listed off a bunch of last names and drew imaginary lines in the air with his index finger.

"And on my mother's side, the Daireauxs, who came from Monfort…"

Mom nodded at each name. There's nothing she enjoys more than putting a name (and an address) to a face. She recently told me that not only does she go around asking who's married to whom, but she also writes down the information in a little velvet notebook that she keeps with her jewelry. In a sudden fit of excitement, she told the ambassador that she too had her family tree made and got back a "colossal cloud, full of names."

I looked at her, gobsmacked. She had done herself in and didn't realize it. She kept on talking without even considering the inevitable question. When she finally paused for air, the ambassador asked her kindly:

"And what is your maiden name?"

Mom hunched. She blushed. Imploded.

"Oh, no, no," she said folding onto herself like a scared armadillo. "You wouldn't know them."

Her body spoke for her, gravity tugging at her posture. She was mumbling so much that the ambassador had to insist.

"Excuse me? I didn't catch that."

"Tabulnik. Forget it, it's Russian. You wouldn't know them, the Tabulniks."

A sadder origami I had never seen.

When we went back to our room, there was a sign with our names on the door, like in maternity wards after a baby is born. "Welcome Raquel and Ema."

"Look at that, they wrote Raquel instead of Elena," I told her.

No one knows Mom by her first name. When she moved to Buenos Aires, she thought Raquel lacked luster and started introducing herself as Elena, which was classier. Since then, my aunt Sara calls her "sweetie" because she could never bring herself to use her sister's middle name.

No one knows Mom by her maiden name either. Even though she never married Dad, she still goes by Elena Sagasti, and her naked ring finger is never not a nuisance because, legally, Elena Sagasti doesn't exist. At the supermarket, when the cashier asks for her ID, the names don't match: her credit card says Elena Sagasti, but her ID says Raquel Elena Tabulnik. Years ago, at a Davos convention for entrepreneurs' wives, her nametag said Raquel Tabulnik. "Look, Elena, you have someone else's tag," a surprised acquaintance told her when she came over to say hello. Mom gave no explanation. She didn't tell her that in addition to Elena Sagasti she is also Raquel Tabulnik. She laughed awkwardly and shrugged it off.

After three days of detox, we took the same route through hills and weeping willows back to Buenos Aires. A bright blue sky served as backdrop. Mom slept until we got to the first tollbooth.

"Here, let me pay for it," she said, searching for the envelope she uses as a wallet. "I want to get rid of some old bills. Here you go, pay with this," she said handing me some beat-up cash.

Halfway back, I asked her about the chronic stress group meetings with the Adventist pastor.

"Should we stop for oranges?" she replied.

On the side of the road, countless signs advertised a good deal on oranges. We bought three bags. We later stopped for avocados, farm eggs, olive oil, and preserved peppers. Mom asked for every price twice. She's never gotten used to being rich. With less than sixty miles left, I asked her again about the group meetings.

"Everyone shared what they were stressed about, and the pastor gave us advice."

"And?"

"It was a mixed group. This one woman, for example. She lives around the block from us, you know her? She said someone in her family was very ill. We all thought it was her son or her husband. But it turned out it was her daughter-in-law who's anorexic, go figure. She doesn't like her because she lies in bed all day and doesn't take care of her children, this woman's grandkids."

"And what did the pastor say?"

"It was good. He told her she needed to stop thinking about her daughter-in-law. At the core, all you have is yourself, no one else. That's the unfortunate truth. But the woman was so clueless she didn't even listen. The pastor said it loud and clear. We are at the center of our own lives, no one else."

"And you?"

"What about me?"

"What did you talk about?"

Mom delayed her answer by sneezing.

"Well, first we had to write our stressors on a piece of paper. I wrote down making decisions I don't know how to make, like buying investment bonds or not. I also wrote not being able to solve computer problems. That stresses me out. And boredom."

"Boredom?"

"Yes, and don't tell me I can fix that by going to the movies, because you know that's not true."

"You do realize that's all pretty stupid, right?"

She laughed.

"Please don't tell me you read that list out loud."

"No, of course not."

"So then what did you say?"

Mom put her hand on her pigeon chest, caressed her little secret, and set it free:

"I said I identified with Borges's famous quote: 'I have committed the worst sin that can be committed. I have not been happy.'"

There was a nostalgic look on her face.

"How come you weren't happy?"

"It was a combination of a lot of small things, what do I know. I feel like I've never done anything."

"You were a doctor, started a family, raised two daughters…"

"I never dared let go, I was always a bit scared. I did what I had to do, but it didn't amount to much. Sara wakes up every morning and says triumphantly 'Another glorious day!' But I think 'Ugh, another day.'"

"And what would you have liked to do?"

"I never knew. I don't know, Ema. That's enough. Should we stop for some coffee?"

We didn't. Mom put on the radio. While she slept, I got myself worked up wondering if my life didn't also revolve around unfulfilled desires and coulda, shoulda, wouldas. I realized I wasn't well-suited for happiness either.

I remembered Mom's conversation with the ambassador and thought about branches made brittle by root rot. I imagined freighters crossing the ocean, crammed with unintelligible languages, with sepia shawls, skirts, and berets, and I wondered from which of these marine creatures disembarked those two Russian farmers, my ancestors.

I too need to travel back in time to understand what I'm made of—families, like all other things, transform into some version of what they used to be. Psychoanalysts speak of an intergenerational subconscious transmission of latent issues, resolved and unresolved. No one becomes who they are in a void. My mother's side leaves a smudgy trace, floating somewhere.

We leave the hotel in Santa Rosa early in the morning and set out to Macachín. Route 35 goes up and down a hazy plain. The windows mist up. I am driving. In the backseat, Sara is on the phone with someone from town and introduces herself as Beatriz, to my surprise.

In La Pampa, everyone knows her by her middle name. She never stopped coming back. "I like it here," she says, opening her hands like a preacher. She still runs my grandfather's salt lake.

"Here, I'm Beatriz. After a while, my aunts and uncles, grandparents, and friends all left, and new people started calling me that," she explains.

Sitting next to me, with her eyes closed, Mom smiles. She stopped being a Tabulnik to become a Sagasti. Her sister stopped being Sara to become Beatriz. Name changes keep me up at night. There's nothing funny about becoming someone else; it confuses people, especially yourself. Like those women who lie so much about their age they just forget what their birthdate is. Our bodies change, so do our ideas and fears, but names provide a common thread. There's no need for entanglements. Once, at a café, I tried being someone new. When they asked for my name, I said Tamara, but then I didn't react when they called for me. They had to scream the name three times.

When Macachín starts appearing on the road signs, Mom asks me to go slower.

"Slow down, Ema, please slow down."

Mom rearranges her position on the seat and places her hand on the window, as if touching the past. The morning's pallor still hasn't cleared.

Our first stop is the town's motor club. A German Shepherd welcomes us. He sniffs Mom, who is petrified. Don't let them smell your fear, they say, but easier said than done. Sara knows her way around town. She claps for him to come and pets his snout.

"Who's a good boy?" she asks him. The dog follows her around wagging his tail.

The motor club is in a white colonial-style building with a red-tiled gable roof. It's abandoned. The windows are boarded up, their green color peeling off. The pump is rusted. Looks like something out of an indie movie, Mom's favorite kind.

"The motor club used to be *the* place," Sara says. "We would drive all the way here down the dirt main road just to hang out. Remember, sweetie? It used to have nice leather chairs and a huge fireplace."

The wind blows, and the branches of a eucalyptus tree cast whimsical shadows on Mom, who is reminiscing about every corner of the club. The old dirt road triggers the memory of her friend Guillomía, a classmate she admired because once for a school assignment he wrote a report on a dazzling police story. It was all fiction.

"He died on that road a few years after that, biking. He fell and hit his head against a rock while showing a friend how he'd learned to ride with no hands," she tells us. The universe is absurd everywhere.

We go back to the car, and in less than a mile we see the town's new entrance, an amorphous geometrical structure painted in bright yellow.

"MACACHÍN," it announces in big block letters. To me, this town is a faraway corner of the planet.

"Population: 5465," I read the sign out loud.

"Can't believe they don't round it off. Do you think it's updated every year?" asks Julia.

"Of course not. It's always the same number," Sara says.

Exiting the roundabout, I lower my window and start down a straight paved road.

"We're here. Slow down, Ema."

I do as I'm told because all of a sudden, I realize: Mom is returning home.

It's Sunday, and Macachín looks like a ghost town. I put on the blinker to make a turn, and Mom and Sara laugh at me. There are no other cars around. We park in front of a dilapidated house with exposed brick and plaid curtains. Julia brings her camera. She wants a record of everything.

"This used to be Uncle Isaac's house. Every time we visited, he gave us candy from a crystal jar," Sara tells us. "Then he moved to the big city in Bahía Blanca."

On the sidewalk, the roots of trimmed trees poke through the stone tiles in several spots, as if trying to break free from their claustrophobic confines. Bare branches grow from their stumps, brittle claws holding up the passing of time that threatens to knock everything down. We start walking, and names, anecdotes, and characters appear as if by magic. A crowd of memories greet Mom and Sara.

"Look, Ema, you were right," Mom says. "The streets are dusty, just like you told Antonio. But I swear they used to be white. Or am I wrong, Sarita? The years have made them filthy." With her foot, she traces a half circle in the dirt of the sidewalk.

Down the block from Isaac's house there is a more modern Western Union sign. The wind makes it swing and whistle. It's the post office. Next to it is the police station.

"The chief of police, the post office manager, and the doctor were the most respected people in town," Sara explains. "When the first dentist moved here, the town threw him a welcome reception, imagine that! It was as if the governor himself were coming." She sounds proud, but she seems unaffected by nostalgia.

"Don't forget the pharmacist, Sarita. He was also important, worthy." Mom uses air quotes when she says worthy.

Julia, Sara, and Mom walk arm in arm; a chain that takes up the width of the sidewalk. I'm a few steps behind. Then we arrive at the house of Zeyde León and Babbe. That's what they called their grandma Irene. Not Bubbe, Babbe.

"One night, as we were on our way back from celebrating the New Year," Sara recounts, "Babbe leaned out of this very window and told us that Zeyde was short of breath. He died the next day. For years, we didn't celebrate New Year's Eve because it was the anniversary of his death."

Ahead of us is the new affordable housing, a charmless residential complex.

"What an eyesore! Architects have no right doing something so hideous. They should respect a town's identity," Mom says.

"It's so that everyone can have a roof over their head, sweetie. I thought you were a communist," Sara tells her.

"It's still an eyesore."

The proliferation of identical houses gives me vertigo. We take a detour to walk around the park, and we end up by the house of Doctor Laspiur, who came from a long lineage of renowned medical professionals in Buenos Aires.

"He was the idiot of the family, that's why he was sent here," Mom explains.

In this town, rumors are reliable construction material. Street names, on the other hand, are merely ornamental. Things are "around the block from the school," "right next to the post office," "by the store," "two houses down from Gaviot's place," "across the street from Agulnik's."

On the next corner is the Dr. Theodor Hertzl Israeli Hall, the place for all major events. Mom was four when they gathered here to celebrate the declaration of the establishment of the State of Israel.

"I remember it because kids can tell when something is really important, and also because Dad was still in great health then," she says.

The Hall is now a bright orange color that seems out of place, until two blocks later we come across the same color on the walls of Kiwi, the town's disco.

When we walk by the school, Mom gets emotional. The classroom combines two of her subjects: childhood and knowledge. From Monday to Friday, Mom and Sara wore a white smock and a pair of Mary Janes to go to school. Mom remembers the day the teacher asked who wrote *Hamlet* and she raised her hand up high, lifting herself from her seat and sticking her neck out to answer. The teacher called her.

"Robespierre!" replied Mom.

The correct answer was of course Shakespeare, which she pronounced "Shakespierre," ergo the mistake.

"So embarrassing!" she tells us, with a voice that unfolds like a rose. Then she adds that she finished the year with honors anyway.

Mom wasn't at Antonio's latest school play. On our way out, she congratulated him and wished him good luck. But when her grandkid, who had the leading role, asked her why she wasn't coming, she just told him she was busy. That was it. Then she went back to her room.

When we arrived at the school, the gym was overflowing with mothers, pulled together as if by magnetism. I stood in a corner, at a safe distance from them. Meanwhile, the music started playing. Antonio searched for me from the stage, squinting. When he looked over my corner, I raised my hand and waved so he could see me. But he didn't. He continued combing the crowd with his eyes until someone made his face brighten up. I understood he wasn't looking for me but for a friend, who waved from the audience.

When the event was over, I looked for him to say goodbye. He gave me a quick kiss and ran back to the other kids.

"Antonio, tie your shoes, you're going to hurt yourself!"

He froze, looked down at his feet and shrugged. Then he went back to running.

It wasn't always like this. In preschool, he would not let go of me. It was a scene at drop-off for six months. Now I embarrass him, the same way my mother embarrassed me. The other mothers were better. She wasn't like Vicky's mom, who dressed her as a showgirl (red feather boa and fishnets included) for a costume party in elementary school. No, Mom wasn't like that. Instead, she took me over to her friend's house, who only had sons. We raided her smelly trunk full of rags, and she finally dressed me as Puss in Boots. She was also not like Cata's mom, who made brownies and smoothies for us. Whenever I had friends over and I complained there was nothing to eat, Mom opened the fridge and said: "What do you mean there's nothing to eat? Here's some spinach pie, a banana, half a hardboiled egg." Sometimes she didn't even have to do or say anything; her mere presence embarrassed me: seeing her at the beach in a one-piece swimsuit instead of a bikini, like everyone else wore, or at parties, with blue mascara clumped on her lashes. She was forty but looked older. Dad was the one who elevated her. Told her what to wear, what shoes to buy, what car to drive. He polished her. But Dad was always at work, and without him, Mom became lackluster, like tarnished silver. She was oblivious to how beautiful she was. Me too. I treated her with contempt, I dismissed her, I wanted to be an orphan. Then I grew up.

We move through town slowly. Some houses appear worn by time. Mom looks around with the same face she makes when she forgets someone's name. "What a hassle," she always says. "I have it on the tip of my tongue, but I can't remember." Sara tells us about some of the neighbors whose houses she recognizes: Nudelman owned a convenience store; the Stenfelets were goyim and later sold their place to the Raskins, who were Jewish; Galinsky was a scrap merchant who "bought and sold junk;" Mrs. Rentería was also a goy, and a piano teacher; Uncle Gregorio used to threaten them as kids with his belt; and Aunt Deidamia had facial hair, according to Mom.

"She was lovely, what does it matter if she had a moustache?" Sara defends her.

"She was a busybody," replies Mom without any further explanation.

The synagogue, or rather, the shul, is abandoned. Through a broken window, I can see a fabric cover with an embroidered Hebrew inscription over the Torah and some other books—the only surviving items. There are almost no Jews left in Macachín.

Across the street is a man with a heavy bone structure and a prominent nose.

"Sara Beatriz!" he yells at my aunt, raising his hand.

It's Saúl Guerstein, a childhood friend who never left. He crosses the street and kisses us hello.

"These are Julia and Ema, my nieces," Sara introduces us. "And here she is, my sweetie. You remember my sister Raquel, no?"

Mom squints and looks at him as if he were a museum piece, hard to decipher.

"You still live here?" she asks him, skeptical. Saúl doesn't pay attention to her and continues talking with Sara, who asks him about the convenience store.

"You mean Festa's bodega, the one by Roztein's place? It closed last year, but I think you're mistaking it for the old store that only opened on Saturdays," he explains.

Saúl has all the answers; the town doesn't forget. He looks at my belly.

"Boy or girl?" he asks me while pulling on his ear.

"Girl," I say.

Mom wants to say something. She looks him straight in the eye but doesn't speak. We say goodbye and he disappears down the empty street.

The last house we visit belonged to Mom and Aunt Sara. Nothing stands but a couple of walls and a cracked concrete floor taken over by weeds. Julia goes in to take some pictures and gets thistles all over her shoelaces. Mom touches some little holes on the wall.

"Look, Sarita! You know what these are from?" Then she tells us: "Here's where that ridiculous painting of a flower vase was, our only artwork. Every so often it fell down, and we had to hang it up again."

Sara sketches what the house used to be like: three bedrooms, one bathroom, a large hallway, and the kitchen on the other end. Powered by her memory, she puts up brick and limestone walls, but I can only visualize the unbearable sight of the ruins. I'm startled by how easy homes crack and collapse, just like that.

Next to our abandoned home stands the house of Doña Rosa and Don Julián, still intact.

"Don Julián couldn't swallow pills. He tried taking them with gulps of water, but there was no way. He stuck his tongue out to show us, he just couldn't do it," Mom tells us. "I must have been five and was so intrigued. It was unbelievable. I can't swallow them either, you know? I guess I inherited that from Don Julián," she says laughing out loud.

The only place that's open for lunch is the cafeteria inside the bus station. Mom and Julia order just a coffee. Sara and I, a sandwich with chips. The other tables are empty. When the food arrives, Julia gets hungry and wants to try some of our chips. And then some more.

"So good, right?" she says, taking another chip.

"Oh, let me try one," Mom says.

When we're done, the table is full of crumpled greasy napkins.

"Should we go to the cemetery? It's only like a mile away, on the other side of town," Sara suggests. She leaves a tip almost as big as the entire check.

"Sarita, it's too much," Mom says.

My aunt ignores her.

The entrance is a wrought iron double door. It features two Stars of David and is chained shut. Right next to it is a shack from which the groundskeeper emerges. A dirty bandana covers his head. He's wearing tattered espadrilles and mud-caked baggy pants. It's impossible to know how old he is exactly. Sara gives him a handshake and some cash. He takes out a key and opens the padlock for us while muttering something to himself. We go in.

"I always thought the cemetery was huge, can't believe how tiny it really is!" Mom says, surprised.

It's just one walled-up block. Men on one side, women on the other. The first grave we find belongs to their zeyde. On his tombstone rest four small stones. "It's a way of honoring the dead, of showing that someone was here visiting," Sara explains. "Compared to flowers, stones are basically eternal. It's the Jewish take on death. The body might rot, but the soul is an evergreen tree."

"I don't know what the soul is. Might as well be one of those affordable housing buildings," Mom says.

Julia reads: "León Tabulnik died on January 1st 1952, at the age of 78. Your wife, children, grandchildren, and great-grandchildren will always remember you."

I look at the tombstone and think that even though Zeyde León didn't have any great-grandchildren when he died, Julia and I were born with the responsibility of honoring his memory, so here we are in the face of immortality's useless glory. There's also a black and white photograph of León, who came from Ukraine. It's the portrait of a man with a terrifying likeness to Mom—a suffocating resemblance. Where does a family start and end?

"Our zeyde was so shabby," Mom tells us. "Every Friday we had dinner at his place, and our mother forbade us from touching anything because the house was just nasty. Babbe wouldn't clean because she said she didn't belong there. Her home was far away; she lived in the past."

The sun no longer warms us. The wind whistles through the cypress trees and lullabies the dead. We visit the tombstones of Babbe, Aunt Deidamia, and Rosa, their neighbor. All these familiar faces are like strangers to me. Like in those dreams where you are walking among friends and family that don't look like friends and family.

We can't find the graves of our grandparents Abraham and Natalia anywhere.

"They're buried at La Tablada Cemetery, in Buenos Aires," explains Sara. "Despite spending their whole lives here, they didn't want to be buried in town. Dad used to say one can only rest in someone else's house. And since we were already living in the city, it was also easier to make the arrangements there. Let's go, there's nothing left to see here."

We go back to town, and right before the sun disappears, we drive by the train station. We park the car, but only Mom and I get out. Julia and Sara stay inside, they're cold.

The station, with a British-style platform, is abandoned. An announcement posted on the ticket office reads: *The last F.C. Roca passenger train to B. Blanca passed through Macachín on August 27th, 1976 at 15:00.*

Mom's eyes fill up. She takes a handkerchief out of her purse and pats her tears dry. We walk in silence. She is one step ahead, low-spirited, shrinking like Alice in Wonderland. The station is an open-air museum, an accumulation of obsolete railway objects: a luggage scale, an emergency handbrake, a blackboard. Mom shakes her head slowly.

"This kills me. I can't," she says, and a wave of images fill her mouth. "We came to the station to see the trains pass by. We even wore white gloves and all, like Sara told you. Then we stopped by Alonso's ice-cream parlor, putting everything on Dad's tab, and then bought something at the sewing shop. Actually, we never bought anything because we had no money, we just looked. We rode our bikes back home at night, and after dinner, when the grownups talked business, us kids met by the streetlight on the corner, where there were always beetles. Under that cone of light, we used a stick to turn them upside down and see their little legs move. That was it, we didn't need anything else. We didn't question anything. We were happy. We just didn't know it."

Back in the car, we cross the tracks and drive down the cobblestone roads. Up in the sky, a moon so full, too rich. Mom says she doesn't recognize the houses on this side of town because this is where the Germans lived, but Sara corrects her:

"No, sweetie, this is where their employees lived. You distort things. Here's where Joselevich lived, for example, that crazy guy who forecasted the weather. And also Ezquiaga, the town thief."

Mom is not paying attention. She clings to her distortions to survive.

The next morning, I have breakfast alone in the dining room of our hotel. Warming my hands on a steaming cup of coffee, I remember the dream I had: a stormy wind came in and blew away my freckles, wrinkles, blackheads. I looked in the mirror and had a plastic face, no traits, no features.

Through the large window I see golden beams of light piercing the clouds. Mom comes in with a folded newspaper in hand.

"Good morning, Ema, how did you sleep?"

"Fine. It's hard with my belly. You?"

"I woke up in the middle of the night and couldn't go back to sleep, so I started reading this newspaper I found in my room's closet. Listen to this column about Fellini."

She sits down and reads aloud. The column is about this woman Fellini comes across at the park; she's all wet from the rain. And also about how he prefers to sit in front of his therapist and eat strudel instead of lying on the couch.

"I can't think of anyone more different to me than Fellini. Getting caught in the rain? Sitting face to face with my therapist? What nonsense!" Mom says, amused.

She's clear-headed. Me too, so I take my chance.

"What was Grandma Natalia like?" I ask.

"Mom? She spent her days in the kitchen but never wanted us to learn how to cook."

Not only does my mother not cook, she also learned to avoid anything useful like the plague. She prefers visiting museums and memorizing operas. I've inherited some of that. I can't turn on the water heater, but I can recognize a supporting actor in any movie. I'm a faithful copy of her useless skills.

"Mothers are weird," I tell her.

"So weird!"

Mom pours herself some coffee and looks for one of the sweetener packets she carries in her purse. As she searches through her stuff, she starts taking things out and putting them on the table. Among several letterhead documents, there's a picture. I take it without asking for permission. It's Dad, in the living room at home. He's sitting; a whisky in one hand, a cigar in the other. I forgot he smoked, and I feel guilty about forgetting the full story of what he represented. Dad loved us in that distant way parents loved their children a century ago. We didn't kiss or wave hello. I don't remember how we said hello. Mom had a similar relationship with him—a mix of fascination and terror—that only let up a bit when he got sick.

"Your dad was great," she says when I give her back the picture.

None of us were with him when he died. Not Mom, or Julia; not me. It happened in the room where Antonio now sleeps and where before him, I had. Miriam, the nurse who was taking care of him, would let out a nervous laugh whenever she didn't understand what she was being asked to do. Dad left a fat farewell check for her in his desk drawer. He had enough time for things like that. When Mom gave her the check, she asked Miriam how it happened.

"How what happened?"

"His death."

"He let out a sigh, different from the others, and lay still. Frozen," she replied with her eyes wide open. Then, she shrieked and said she had to go because she was about to miss her train. Days later, Mom told me that in that last sigh, Dad had let out his soul. I told her I didn't know what the soul was and neither did she.

I would have liked to see him one last time, but then I guess I would've wanted one more time after that. Not Mom. She would have preferred never finding out about how futile Dad's body had become.

"Are you afraid of dying?" I ask her while pouring myself more coffee.

"Life, death, loneliness… people sure like to philosophize about that! But please, dying is the most natural thing in the world. And everyone is still so surprised when someone dies: a friend, an uncle, a celebrity. Even worse if it's a young person who dies. They become like demigods, like there's any merit in dying young."

She takes a long pause, then adds:

"What's difficult, truly difficult, is surviving someone."

Mom puts the photo back on the table. I turn it around to see it again and discover that, in the background, by chance, is also Juvencia, who is looking straight into the camera. She's wearing the blue uniform with white polka-dots. Her feet are cut off from the picture, but I can almost hear her flip-flopping around.

"Do you remember Juvencia?" I ask my mother.

"Of course, how could I not? She took over the entire house! She was always pestering me about stuff I forgot to get her at the store. Luckily, she left pretty quickly."

"She didn't leave, you fired her. The day I started walking again, you fired her."

"Really? Not sure that's what happened. Is that what happened?"

Juvencia, *che mitãkuña*, I think, and I ask for her forgiveness wherever she is.

Mom stares into nothing, like she's lost or forgotten something. Then, she says:

"I remember your accident. Do you?"

The question stops me in my tracks.

"Some things about it, yes."

I don't specify what things. I don't tell her about my archeology of loneliness while bedridden. I don't mention that last image—her in the car, just looking.

"I remember it with a terrifying sharpness. I remember the fall," she says, her eyes stuck on the window, paralyzed.

"How can that be? I was alone when I fell."

Suddenly, I'm cold. I hug myself, for shelter.

Mom raises her eyebrows and takes a breath. She grows a couple of inches until she exhales through her nose. I think she won't say anything else, but this time she chooses to confess:

"Whenever I got too overwhelmed at home, in that big stone house in Mar del Plata, I needed to get away, and I took refuge in the car. I considered starting it, but I never did. I just sat there. In moments like that, I couldn't care less about things. On the day of your accident, the car was parked outside, right across the street from the house. When I saw you going up that ladder... I don't know what I thought would happen, it's been so many years... The reasonable thing to do would have been to get out of the car and scream at you to stop because it was dangerous. I thought about it, I think I did. But I didn't do it. And then the ladder started moving."

I remain silent. Mom and I never knew how to talk to each other. She hides what she thinks in such a remote corner that when she speaks she can only do so in trivialities. "I need to talk to you," she announces, but then she hardly ever says anything worthwhile. Except for now.

"When I came closer and found you passed out, I froze. A trickle of blood started coming out of your nose... then another one, out of your ear... I didn't dare touch you. It was terrifying. I could feel my heart throbbing in my stomach, in my hands. Something irreparable had happened, that's all I knew. I got this feeling here, in my chest, that never left me. Up until that day, you had been a child. From then on, we ceased to understand each other, don't you think? At least I never could... I don't know... something broke between us."

A galloping sadness takes over me. The certainty of knowing that she had let me fall, just as I suspected all these years, breaks me. Deep down, I always knew. Just this once, I would have preferred Mom to deny everything. Under the table, I ball my hands into fists, my fingernails sticking sharply into my palms. I bite my tongue. I hold my breath underwater.

"A man who was walking by and saw you fall called the ambulance. I didn't thank him, I couldn't snap out of it, I was paralyzed. Fortunately, we never saw him again. It's one of the few people who's known all these years what kind of mother I am."

"And what kind is that?" I ask her with a broken voice that holds back a deep anger—the deep anger of love.

I drink my coffee, scalding hot, and I burn my mouth and throat. Tears fill my eyes, and I blink quickly to dry them. Mom raises her mug, attempts a half smile, and hastily ends her confession:

"A bad one. Like all mothers."

I look at her and I hate her. For the first time, I hate her. Because I'm different from her, and the same. Something hard hurts my throat and holds back my crying. Fury burns my face.

Sara comes into the room wearing a huge maroon bag and lipstick in a matching shade. She's ready for whatever the day may bring.

"How are you, girls? What a gorgeous day! Sweetie, there you go, you forgot your glasses in the room again. You never change, do you?" she says to Mom.

"No, no one does," she replies, curt.

Mom looks at me from the corner of her eye. I look away. I'm having trouble breathing, like a fish writhing and gasping, freshly out of water. I crack my knuckles. It's a nervous habit since childhood. Not many know about it. I usually have it under control. I don't want my knuckles to get deformed, to expose me like that.

"We need to go pick up the boxes," Sara says.

"What?" Mom interrupts.

My head is somewhere else too, and I'm having trouble coming back to reality. I can't think. I'm overcome with memories.

"The boxes. We're here for some boxes. Remember I got a call from city hall, sweetie?"

I rub my eyes and see a bunch of twinkling red, black, and white spots, like a dumb screensaver, until I manage to deflect and focus my sight. I also forgot about the boxes. To me, they were just an excuse to come to Macachín. Now, as I break my toast in half trying to butter it, I dream that these boxes could fill the gaps in my trail of breadcrumbs. I swallow in a hurry. It's a lot to digest.

"Let me get the check and we'll get going, shall we? Julia's on her way down," Sara tells us.

As she walks away, I come to myself, and the world around me settles down.

"What about you, Mom? Are you paying for anything this trip?" I attack her suddenly, my lips pressed indicating reproach. "Sweetie. That nickname sure does fit you. Sweet little sweetie," I tell her with an unfriendly cackle. I can't think of anything else to say to her.

It drives me crazy that I can't insult her as the grown woman I am and instead I do it as if I were eleven. I need to hurt her. Incredibly, I succeed. She turns white and looks for Sara, but she is gone already. Mom opens her mouth and closes it. A wave of guilt comes over me. Mom looks at the letterhead documents still on the table and quickly puts them back in her purse. Her hands are shaking.

"What's wrong? Are you okay?"

"Nothing. It's nothing," she says. And then, immediately after, as if the last minute hadn't happened, she adds: "Your coffee must be getting cold. Drink up and let's go."

When Julia comes down, we walk with Sara a few blocks to the warehouse. Mom prefers to drive, alone. It's Monday, and the town looks a bit more animated than yesterday: a dog prances down the street, a woman pushes her shopping cart. I drag my feet, my hands are in my pockets. The cold condenses our breath. The sun doesn't warm nor dazzle, even if I stare at it.

"What do you think is in those boxes? Did someone in the family ever work for city hall?" asks Julia.

"Not that I know of. I have no idea how or why those boxes ended up there," Sara replies.

I imagine a manuscript by Uncle Isaac or Uncle Gregorio that records and casts memories of the past. Piles of envelopes tied with ribbon. Letters full of reproaches and voices, the building blocks of relatives. Or maybe a great novel with an omniscient narrator that can explain the parts of those other lives I don't understand.

The warehouse is a huge metal building with a half-open sliding door. Marta, the woman who talked to Sara on the phone about the boxes, is waiting for us outside. Her hair is whiskey blonde, she wears her glasses on the tip of her scrunched up nose, and her skirt has a print of flowers that look like stains.

"Wait here, please. I'll bring out the box," she tells us as soon as we go in, with a warm voice that doesn't match her stocky body type. I was expecting the hoarse voice of a math teacher.

"I thought there were several boxes?" Julia asks.

"No, yours is only one. Let me get it. We had to throw out so many others because we didn't have anyone's contact information, entire families that just disappeared without a trace."

"What was this warehouse for?" I ask.

"A bit of everything, a mix of things people didn't want to get rid of but also didn't want to ever look at again. We need to empty it because it's going to be knocked down. They're building a new gym, with an indoor swimming pool."

While we wait, I see out the window a flock of sparrows performing a choreographed dance up in the sky, soaring and plummeting, writing in cursive.

"Here it is, there you go," Marta says, dragging a box with her feet. It's small but heavy.

Must be the letters, I think. Dozens of letters revealing secrets, infidelities, and fears. I'm the only one in the group who is excited.

"Let me open it!" I say, almost screaming. I squat to take off the lid, my legs spread out like a frog to avoid squashing my belly. No one moves. They're all standing with crossed arms because of the cold. No one talks. Marta joins in on the expectation. The first thing I see are several identical notebooks. My heart beats faster. I knew it, I think.

"I knew it," I whisper.

But then reality hits. The notebooks are filled with numbers.

"They're balance sheets or something like that," I say scanning one after the other, shrugging, crestfallen. I fumble inside the musty and dusty box as if my ancestors could be hiding somewhere in there. The last notebook I find is different from the others. It's smaller, leatherbound, with a letter "A" engraved on the cover. I open it and see no numbers, only text written in blue ink. But the words are illegible, smudged, and after the third page, there's no more writing. I go over paragraph by paragraph and can only make out "...*and beneath her feet there was a sapphire tiled floor, as clear as the sky itself. Yet He did not extend his hand against the princes of the sons...*" I reread it a couple of times, and try as I might, I can't figure it out, I can't even get creative. Sara and Mom neither. Julia takes pictures. Mom grabs one of the notebooks and dusts it off with her coat sleeve.

"Business!" she says.

Sara also grabs one.

"These are Dad's dry goods store balancing sheets. Look at these numbers, sweetie, do you remember these numbers? It was the only thing Dad ever wrote down: numbers," my aunt explains. "And how meticulous he was!"

"Minuscule, rather. Look at those little numbers. They shrunk together. Dad and his numbers," says Mom.

They both give each other a conspiratorial look, and I give up on this foreign territory. I'll never be a part of this town or its people. None of this belongs to me.

Listless, I inspect the notebooks some more, page by page, and inside I find a few old photographs, surviving unintentionally the passing of time. They're portraits of serious people. I speculate that none of these men and women wanted to spoil their posterity with a disingenuous smile, like those that abound now. Or maybe they simply had ugly teeth.

"Do you recognize anyone?" I ask Mom and Sara.

I hand them the stack of photos, and they look at them one by one. They shake their heads.

"No, they must be distant relatives of Mom or Dad," Sara says, indifferent.

When she hands them back, I find a photo of a boy who looks exactly like Antonio, dressed in a coat of the time, boots on his little feet, and a beret on his head. With my eyes still on the picture, I realize I do belong here. We are the ghosts of our ancestors. There is no escaping them. No escaping at all.

"Look! Who does he look like?"

I show Mom the picture. She says nothing.

"Mom, please, he's identical to Antonio. Any idea who it might be? He looks exactly the same!"

"To Antonio? You think? No, I don't think so, Ema."

Mom doesn't know what color Antonio's eyes are. Or what grade he's in, or when his birthday is. If someone were to ask her about her grandson, she'd say he's a nice and happy boy, or some other trifle suitable for kids between four and twelve years old. She doesn't pay much attention to people because she pities everyone. She doesn't tire of saying poor Antonio, poor Ema, poor everyone.

"And you, Sarita? Do you know who he is?"

She doesn't either. Julia takes a picture of the picture but doesn't say anything.

Mom and Sara sign a few release forms for the box. We put it in the trunk of the car, turning it into another abandoned warehouse. Without asking anyone about it, I keep the picture of the other Antonio. It's in my purse. It's mine.

"Don't you want to visit the salt lake before going back?" Julia asks.

"I'd be happy to, it's like ten miles from town. What do you think, sweetie?" Sara says.

"Sure, but then it's straight to Buenos Aires, I don't want us driving after dark."

The road to the salt lake is bad. It's been damaged by flooding from the river and the trucks that come and go in the summer to exploit it. A hill of Roman cassia trees hogs the landscape on both sides. A parade of clouds rides with us. We go through several farm gates until we reach one with a wooden sign and the name painted in white: La Beatriz. Sara smiles big, showing her teeth and gums, and gets out to open the lock. Then she asks for a picture next to the sign. She poses with her neon yellow blouse and silver pants, her puffy hair, her open hips, and her fists on her waist. The millionaire with her salt kingdom in the background.

"Isn't this place amazing?" she asks as we move forward through a field of hostile bushes.

Then a lake appears. The four of us walk to the shore. It's not deep or wide. A rundown wire fence cuts it in the middle.

"Between November and March, the water turns to salt. It's beautiful," Sara tells us. She speaks of the salt lake as if it were an enchanted land. She used to come here as a girl with her father and then kept coming as an adult until it became her place in the world.

During the summers when I was a kid, Mom used to tell us that Aunt Sarita was here, and that she'd bring us one day, but she never did. I imagined a place in the middle of nowhere, a shack next to a big white lake. I'm surprised by how much this image looks like my fantasy. The only thing missing is the shack. Sara let it go under a few years ago because it was too much work. Now every time she comes, she stays in town.

Mom never liked it here. When their parents died, Sara renewed the lease on the lake, bought a piece of land next to it, and made it a profitable venture. Mom never came back.

"I remember it as a hellish place. When the sun came out it was nice, but bright red and devastating, like hell. A visual oxymoron," she says with her hands in her pocket.

Sara smiles and replies:

"Too bad you can't appreciate it, sweetie, because

aside from being beautiful, this salt lake is also a goldmine."

"Really? How much?"

"You have no idea," Sara says in a neutral tone of voice.

"But how much?" Mom insists, tensing.

"Sweetie, what kind of question is that? You never cared about any of this."

"Because I never made a dollar out of it. Isn't it half mine too?"

Sara frowns and sighs. Horrible wrinkles mark her forehead. She turns serious. Mom keeps looking at her, stubborn.

"Do you need a reminder of how things went down, sweetie?"

Mom wavers and lowers her head. She doesn't need any reminders.

Julia once explained to me what had happened: when our grandfather Abraham went bankrupt, Sara, who was seventeen at the time, came from Buenos Aires to Macachín, went to the bank, and told the manager that from that day onward she'd be in charge of her father's accounts. In addition to wearing her best dress, she also took Mom, who was fourteen, for effect. She nailed it. The bank promised to continue wiring her money under the condition that she pay a third of the debt. Sara then decided to do a selloff. First, she printed some flyers listing everything that was up for sale and then she cleared everything out. "She sold an entire warehouse full of junk, useless things of no value, flatware and tools, I don't know what exactly, but she sold it all and saved everyone from bankruptcy," Julia told me. She'd heard it from Mom.

In order to pay off the rest of Abraham's creditors, Sara dropped out of law school and for years dedicated her life to two things: working the salt lake and caring for her sister. She and Mom had moved to Buenos Aires, where they shared a two-bedroom rental. They slept in one room and sublet the other. To women only. Sara traveled to La Pampa every three weeks. Mom started med school. Not because of vocation or tradition. Even less that she wanted to save lives. She did it because she wanted to be *someone*. When she graduated, Sara sold a wagonload of salt and gave all that money to her sister, along with a bottle of champagne, which they drank together.

With the money, Mom rented and furnished her own studio apartment downtown, where she set up her office and her home. During the day, she placed an exam table in the center of the room and saw patients. At night, she moved it against the wall, laid a tablecloth on it, and used it for dinner, which she always ate alone. She slept on the couch where patients, separated by a folding screen from the "office," waited for their appointments.

With her sister on her own, Sara went back to school. She graduated at thirty-six.

When Julia told me this story, I realized how much more she knew than me about Mom's life. The only thing

I could say about that period was that Mom wasn't good at the family business and worked as a doctor until she met Dad. Whereas Julia would have specified that the business was a salt lake with an annual production of six hundred tons of sodium chloride and that Mom did her dermatology residency at the Hospital de Clínicas, where she then worked for nine years, in addition to the ER at the Hospital Rivadavia while also running her own medical practice, first in her studio and then in a larger apartment downtown.

Every one of the details my sister gave me about Mom dazzled me. Not only because I'm proud of having a mother who studied and dedicatedly practiced a profession I admire, but also because they were details unrelated to her as a mother, but rather as another person. It was the first time I thought about her as someone who overcame adversity once and again, someone who, before becoming a mother, had been other things.

Julia knows where Mom has a bank account, what the name of her primary doctor is, the days when she has bridge lessons. Julia always knew more, but I considered that information incidental. I thought closeness and bonding should run separately and unilaterally from a mother to a daughter, from Mom to me. Now I'm not so sure.

"Come on, it's getting cold," Sara says.

Before going back to the car, I look at the sky's reflection on the lake. I try to imagine Sara's paradise and Mom's hell, but I only see a pool of white water. A pool that says something untranslatable.

We only speak a little on the way back. Julia is driving. I'm in the backseat. I close my eyes, and I try to memorize the stories I heard these days, try to retain the past. I repeat names that no longer name anyone. I tend to idealize what's gone, missing memories not my own. Zeyde's mess, Julián's struggle to swallow his pills, Aunt Deidamia's mustache, Mom yelling *Robespierre*. I see them in slow motion, in sepia, untouchable.

I don't want to stop being a daughter, but I can't be just that. I would like something made solely by me, without any inherited genes. I touch my belly with both hands. The baby kicks. Inside is something of mine, without history, an unscathed legacy. I remember the photo I stole of Antonio's lookalike and the thrill of something new fades.

My phone vibrates. It's Lucas. I don't pick up. I text him that we'll be back in Buenos Aires tonight. Macachín is behind us, vanishing slowly. The road's unchanging landscape cradles me and I fall asleep.

When I wake up, I'm the only one in the car, stopped on the side of the road. It's dark, and it takes me a moment to understand what's happening. Outside, Julia and Sara hold Mom's hair and shoulders while she hunches throwing up. I have never seen her throw up. She spits out something viscous. Tar. Black vomit. Julia sees me in the car and signals me with her hand to stay inside.

"Stay-in-side," she spells out with her lips, no voice.

What in the world? I circle my index finger around my temple to let her know she's crazy. Who does she think she is? I squint my eyes and give her a hateful look, like when I was eight, ten, twelve years old, and I thought I had a secret superpower. She bites her lower lip, annoyed, raises an eyebrow and then looks away. What an idiot. I slam the door getting out of the car, but no one pays attention to me.

Drool strings from Mom's mouth, and I start feeling sick too. Vomiting is contagious, like yawning. Vertigo and boredom, two incurable diseases. I go up to Mom; her eyes are red. Julia puts her arms around her. Sara folds a dirty handkerchief and presses it against her forehead. I'm left out, once again.

"What happened, Sarita?" I ask.

"Nothing, darling. Your mom got carsick. That's it, it's nothing."

I can't see Mom's face, she has her back to me, but something is off. She never throws up. Her shoulders go up and down with every spasm. Julia caresses her hair and calms her down. I'm like a hungry puppy who can't find a spot to nurse. Sara rubs her shoes against the grass to clean off splashes of vomit. Mom and Julia walk back to the car. Only then do I see the sign right in front of us. The name VILLA FOURNIER is crossed out, indicating the end of the town. We just drove across it. Is this place in the middle of nowhere where over fifty years ago my grandparents were killed in a car accident the reason for my mother vomiting? I picture the debris on the asphalt, a bed of broken glass around the wrecked car, and the perfect quietude that follows what's irreversible.

"Let me get you a sweater from the trunk," Julia tells Mom, now on her own, standing by the car. I go near her and touch her arm, but it's hard for me. It doesn't feel natural, so I stop. Mom babbles something.

"What was that, Mom?"

"...br...k..."

I hold her hand.

"Easy, it's ok. It's normal to break down in the face of tragedy, some things you just can't let go of..."

Mom looks up and gives me a desperate, unhinged look.

"I'm broke, Ema. Don't you get it? Broke!" she says, shaking her head. She lets go of my hand and looks for her purse in the car. It's the only thing of hers I could ever look through. She keeps all sorts of nonsense in it. Clumsily, she opens it and takes out those letterhead documents I saw at breakfast. She waves them to my face like a fan.

"I have no money, Ema! I'm broke! Do you understand what I'm saying?! Bankrupt!"

She's simultaneously nervous and euphoric, crying out as if she were at a party. A loud party. Behind her deranged eyes you can see her distress.

Julia and Sara come and hold her. I grab one of those papers at random, like choosing a card for a magic trick, and I see the logo of a bank. I glance at it; there are words I don't understand, underlined figures, and a callous stamp over a signature in blue ink.

"Did you know about this?" I ask, handing the paper to Sara.

She doesn't even look at it.

"Some of it, dear," she replies.

"Yes, and we'll come up with something. Don't worry about it, Mom. Now get in the car," Julia says.

I don't move. I try to fit together pieces that don't fit together. It makes no sense.

"This is why you're falling apart, Mom? Money? With everything you've been through, and you care about money? What's wrong with you?"

She doesn't reply. I laugh with fear and incomprehension until I turn stiff as wood. Mom and I are two unaffiliated units tied together circumstantially.

Julia walks Mom to the backseat. Sara is about to go in the driver's seat, but I take the keys from her, and I sit there instead. I grab onto the wheel, squeezing the leather with both hands. Driving helps me clear my thoughts. It's a habit I got on the road, running over insects. In the rearview mirror I see Mom looking out the window, her head lost in the landscape, faraway. I suddenly see a regular old woman. Not even her intelligence or beauty can hide the signs that she's just like any other mother. What would I think of her if instead of knowing her as my mother I'd had the chance to meet her as a stranger? I understand, finally, that she's not special. She's finite and terribly human.

I press down on the gas pedal, and the speedometer starts moving quickly. No one talks. We get caught in a downpour. The road ahead becomes illegible; I can't see anything. The windshield wipers and my heartbeat are in sync, and I can start putting together the puzzle in my mind. I am driving towards a moment of emotional maturity. In search of an epiphany.

One of the few vivid memories I have of Mom being a mother is when she cut my nails with a little pair of tortoise shell scissors over the gray marble countertop in her bathroom. It was a task only she was able to perform. "Let's go cut your nails," she said, and I spread my fingers like a starfish and offered them to her with blind faith.

Mom tried to stay as far as possible from me. She didn't want to influence me. Children, she once told me, should raise themselves. "Besides, up close everything's ugly. I mean, look at your skin!" she told me after I gave birth to Antonio and my belly filled with stretchmarks.

Julia created another type of family. Not only did she remove the seeds from the grapes for her children, she also peeled them, one by one, until she had enough to fill two mason jars. The night before the beginning of the school year, she spent the entire night labeling their supplies. She never let anyone else pick up the twins from a birthday party. If she couldn't go herself, they didn't go. But she always could.

"I need to go to the bathroom. Can you stop at the next gas station?" my sister asks.

I nod. Lightning strikes against a black background, thunder roars on the horizon. The sky looks cracked.

Where do I fall as a mother? I don't want to stand in opposition. When I took piano lessons, my teacher tried getting me to improvise a melody over a rhythmic base she played in her stereo. "Just play anything on the white keys, you can't go wrong," she said. But I failed, I couldn't create anything of my own, I needed someone else's scores. Some part of that comes back to me now as an echo.

"Darling, please go slower, you can't see anything in this rain," Sara asks me.

I take my foot off the gas pedal, and the speedometer goes back within the speed limit. The rain stops. The clouds open up. The day sees us off with a sky that turns orange, red, violet, until it reaches an unfathomable color. I look at Mom again in the rearview mirror. She seems asleep.

At home, we never celebrated Children's Day. Whenever that day arrived and I insisted on a present, Mom never knew what I was talking about. Yet every Mother's Day, at school, they forced us to make something with clay. For years, I gave my mother an ashtray as a present. It was the only thing I knew how to make. She thanked me and put it away in a drawer. She never needed anything I could offer her. I wonder if she was fair with me. I wonder if I was fair with her. I do some more thinking. Fairness has nothing to do with motherhood. Motherhood has to do with a reliance that is as real as it is accidental. I look at Mom one last time in the rearview mirror and for the rest of the trip I look ahead.

03. The Birth

It took me two days to give birth to Antonio. It wasn't until my third trip to the hospital that they admitted me. I was in labor for fifteen more hours. His birth went through just like in the movies, including heart-wrenching screams and pools of sweat. When they placed my son on my chest, he twisted back like a spring—his eyes still shut, his entire body covered in blood and fluids—and started howling. The separation of our bodies terrified both of us.

My second delivery took only a matter of minutes. I was grocery shopping with Mom when my water broke. She took me to the hospital. The nurse who checked my cervix had cold, red hands. Her fat, butcher-like fingers moved dexterously inside my dark cavities, applying pressure.

"She's coming," she said. "How are you feeling?"

"Nervous," I replied.

A woman's primal scream required the nurse's presence in another room, and she never came back. Lucas was on his way. So was the anesthesiologist. Neither made it on time.

Mom stayed with me until another nurse showed up with the attending doctor. He was a stocky man of few words, precise like a math equation. They put me on a gurney and took me to the delivery room, all stainless steel and fluorescent lighting. It was going to be an unmedicated birth. The contractions were getting closer and more painful, pushing me to the edge of sanity. I wanted someone else to do the work for me. For life to be born elsewhere. No one should be born to a mother.

"Squeeze my hand while you push," said the nurse, "She's coming." She had frizzy hair and wise, dark circles under her eyes. She reminded me of those nurses at the turn of the century who walked the hospital halls with a candle. I shook my head from side to side.

"Where's my mom?" I asked.

"She wanted to wait outside."

My mother is the kind of woman who leaves quietly, without telling anyone that she's leaving, as if she had never been there to begin with. While I was giving birth, I imagined her having coffee in the cafeteria downstairs, oblivious to the servers, the coughing coming from other tables, the clinking of spoons—oblivious to everything. She'd been like that for a while. After the trip to Macachín, even though Sara had taken care of her debt and saved her from bankruptcy, Mom wasn't the same. She didn't want her friends to see her, she didn't want to be looked down on. She couldn't bear the weight of so much shame.

"You're doing great. Push when I tell you to," the nurse instructed me.

I pushed three times. On the fourth, an animal howl erupted from my throat and into the air. I screamed for everything I still don't have words for, and something broke free from my body—once more, and forever.

When they took me to my room, Lucas and Antonio were waiting for me. I looked out the window and noticed it was dark out. I had lost track of time. They had just seen the baby in the nursery. She was brought in a few minutes later in a transparent bassinet, swaddled in a pristine blanket. Her dark hair almost looked blue, her eyes were almond-shaped, and her fists were tightly closed. She was a tiny little maze of light.

Antonio chose her name. He decided on Juana.

"It's like Juan, but with an 'a' at the end," he explained.

There was something off about Lucas. He was biting his lips, his nails.

"Go wash your hands so you can hold your sister," he told Antonio, who hopped his way to the bathroom.

Lucas sat at the edge of the bed, cleared his throat, and said:

"Your Mom is upstairs. She had a stroke."

I felt the room closing in on me. Lucas tried to touch my hair, but I avoided his hand.

"That can't be right. When did this happen? She was with me a moment ago."

"The doctors didn't say much. She's in the ICU. They don't think she'll make it through the night."

He kept talking and moving his hands, but I didn't understand what he was saying. The words and the gestures blended together. It felt like being suspended between two train cars, caught in that violent and deafening space.

"I want to see her. I want to see her now," I interrupted.

"Sara is with her. Julia is on her way," he replied.

I stood up despite the pain—skin hanging from my abdomen, breasts swollen, blood clots coming out of me, and muscles seizing in a barrage of inexplicable little spasms all over.

"I'll go with you. She's in room 303," said Lucas.

"No, you stay with them," I told him, brushing by. Antonio was back from the bathroom and was staring at his sister, mesmerized.

I put on a robe and left the room.

I walked slowly down the maternity ward, decorated with baby blue and pink signs welcoming Santiago, Diego, and Carmela, with knitted booties hanging from some of the doorknobs. I saw nurses dressed in white, coming and going pushing cribs, like calm seagulls gliding over the sea. From one room came the inconsolable wail of a newborn.

I got into the elevator and went to the ICU floor. At the nurses' station, I asked for Elena Sagasti. Without looking up from her cell phone, a nurse with a big, stern mouth announced that visiting hours were over and that only one family member per patient was allowed. I asked her to let me go in just for a second, just to see her. She looked up, noticed my robe and hospital wristband, and opened her eyes wide.

"What are you doing here, momma? Did you get the wrong floor? You can't be here now."

"I was told my mother was here. Please, let me in."

The nurse sighed.

"In and out, understand?" she said, and then added smiling: "What's the name?"

"Elena Sagasti."

"I mean your baby's."

"Oh, I see. Juana. Her name is Juana," I replied.

The nurse stood up and held the double door for me. It opened into a parallel dimension of heartbreak. A deafening sound haunted the place. It was the murmur of ventilators, the beeping of medical equipment. I went into room 303. Sara was sitting on a chair next to the bed, her back to the door. I came closer and brought my hands to my mouth in shock. Mom's body was covered in wires. She was hooked to a monitor showing an irregular line blinking and moving, blinking and moving, accompanied by an electric buzz. I couldn't translate what it was writing.

Sara saw me and smiled the way you smile at hospice patients, with sad eyes and a clenched jaw to keep the smile from falling apart. She didn't say a single word. She had never run out of words with me, but this time there was nothing to be said.

Mom looked sound asleep and ancient; she had aged twenty years in a few hours. A horrible bruise marked her arm where they had put in her IV; her skin was so pale it was almost grey. I took one of her hands in mine and covered it in wet kisses. It was a lot smaller than I remembered, as if it had lost volume. For a while Mom had been getting shorter, her back smaller and body slimmer. Like all old people. A friend of mine always said she didn't like hugging her grandmother because she kept shrinking. The gap between them grew larger every time; it was impossible to calculate her real size. That's what I thought of while I was kissing Mom's hand.

The room didn't have a window, didn't offer a single connection to the outside world. There was no sound either, nothing reminiscent of human life audible over the machine's humming. The ceiling felt extremely low, like a nightmare. I was suddenly dizzy and had to grab onto the bed rails. An alarm went off in another room and I thought it must have been something serious, an emergency requiring much diligence and attention. In our room, nothing moved. The stillness was suffocating. Then a nurse knocked on the door and asked me to leave.

"I got it, dear," Sara told me. "You can go."

It was that brief, that unfathomable. I had no time to be scared, to lose myself, to fall apart. No time for anything. On my way out, a nurse in room 302 was stripping the dirty sheets from an empty bed.

I didn't sleep that night. The baby was crying. I held her close to my chest and walked all around the room. Every time I tried putting her back in the bassinet, she started crying again. I held her and, smelling her hair, whispered the story of a woman once named Raquel who suffered from insomnia. Sleeping pills no longer worked for her, so after the day faded into night, she stayed up late listening to operas or reading about Greek mythology. Other times, she sat cross-legged and spread open volumes of a red encyclopedia all around her until she'd cover the entire wooden floor. She looked up her whole life in dictionaries. As a girl, she had seen her grandparents reading in a Hebrew they didn't understand. They could pronounce the letters and combine them into words, but they did not know what they meant. As for her, she couldn't stand not knowing certain things. If in the middle of lunch someone said a word she'd never heard before, she might very well stand up and go look up "echolalia," "logorrhea," "acme," or "vituperation" in an etymological dictionary. She needed to know where words came from. In various notebooks, with a sharp black pencil, she took down impossible-to-decipher notes; only pharmacists could understand her doctor handwriting. Lines and dots. She even scribbled in the margins, like a crazy person, cramming in definitions and ideas she never went back to. When she finally fell asleep, she never dreamed. Sometimes she said she would have liked to be a teacher, but just thinking about it made her tired. Raquel had wasted all of her energy disguising who she was. She camouflaged herself at gatherings and cocktail parties in order to go unnoticed. Her worst nightmare was standing out. Over the years, she excelled at playing the roles others had assigned her, keeping her secret so well hidden that she ended up deceiving herself. She didn't know where she belonged. For a long time she lived distracted. She went to the movies almost every day, the only place where she allowed herself to cry. She stayed put until the very last credit rolled. Recognizing names was a physical need for her, everywhere. She played cards, took art history classes, and let herself be talked into going on group trips only never to leave her hotel room afterward. She was terrified of having a fall far from home and breaking into a million pieces. If someone told a joke at a dinner party, she asked whoever was sitting close by to explain it to her, and even then, she did not always understand. She never told jokes. She didn't speak any English. She pronounced *Israel* the Jewish way. For Raquel, life didn't pass by in vain, but it didn't make much sense either.

She didn't cook, dance, or play sports. Her biggest talent was the art of being loved, but she was oblivious to it. Even though she was surrounded by people, she almost always felt alone. She once made a list of five women she admired, and she decided those were going to be her friends. She got together with one and didn't know what to talk about. Hell is not other people, she used to say. Hell is oneself. She never knew she had a daughter who was obsessed with her, a daughter who believed that being born to that mother was the one real thing that had ever happened to her—that would keep on happening forever. As an adult, Elena used to say she didn't want anything except for one thing: for someone to read Russian short stories to her in her old age, the same kind her mother had read to her as a child. She had mostly forgotten her mother, but she had arbitrarily held on to a bunch of blurry memories of those snowy stories full of pastures and inheritances—the stories of a lifetime.

My daughter quieted down. I pushed a button and called the nurse. She asked me if I wanted her to take the baby. I said yes. She held out her arms, and I gave her my daughter. Before the door closed behind her, I asked her if she knew anything about my mom. "I don't know who your mother is," she said.

ACKNOWLEDGMENTS

Adriana Riva's work first appeared in English in 2021 in *Columbia Journal* when they published my translation of her short story "Pink Peppercorn" from the collection *Angst* (Tenemos las máquinas, 2017). Alongside the author, I did my first bilingual reading of *Salt* for the PEN America's Women-in-Translation readings series in 2021. Thank you to event organizers and moderators Jenna Tang, Piotr Florczyk, and Nancy Naomi Carlson for selecting this project. Throughout the translation process, I was incredibly lucky to be able to workshop many sections of the book with the Third Coast Translators Collective (TCTC) and the Matemates (Will Morningstar, Nora Carr, and Travis Price): I truly couldn't have done it without your feedback and support. Thank you also to TCTC member Susanna Lang for curating a Jill! Reading Series on YouTube in 2022, where a bilingual reading of an excerpt from *Salt* was included. Thank you to the entire Veliz Books team for trusting me with this novel, and especially to Laura Cesarco Eglin who, in the process of editing the manuscript, became a friend. Thank you to Programa SUR for supporting the translation of Argentine literature, and for financing this publication. Thank you to Rhonda Buchanan for your help with the application. To Sofía Galarce for the cover image and design. To Jennifer Croft and Margarita García

Robayo for your endorsements. To Lisa Katz at *Tupelo Quarterly* and to *Latin American Literature Today* for running excerpts of my translation. To Odelia Editoras, an Argentine women-led independent press, for publishing the novel in Spanish. And thank you to author Adriana Riva for joining me in bilingual readings, for answering my questions, and for writing *La sal*.

D.K.

ABOUT THE AUTHOR

Adriana Riva was born in Buenos Aires in 1980. In 2017, she published the short-story collection *Angst* (Tenemos las máquinas), in 2019 the novel *La sal* (Odelia), and in 2022 the poetry collection *Ahora sabemos esto* (Rosa Iceberg). She co-founded the children's publisher Diente de León, for which she wrote the illustrated books *Entre las hojas que cantan*, *La sartén por el mango*, *Contar Buenos Aires*, and *Sol mayor*. She is the co-editor of the literary magazine *El gran cuaderno*. She has three daughters.

ABOUT THE TRANSLATOR

Denise Kripper is an Argentine literary translator and translation scholar. She is the translation editor at *Latin American Literature Today* and the author of *Narratives of Mistranslation: Fictional Translators in Latin American Literature* (Routledge, 2023). She lives in Chicago, where she is a founding member of the Third Coast Translators Collective.